HARD CLIMB TO HELL

Bullets from below ricocheted off the rock around Cimarron as he climbed up the canyon wall. Flying rock chips cut his skin, sweat stung his eyes, the beat of the blood in his veins drummed in his head and his teeth ground audibly against one another.

Then his groping left hand bent forward at the wrist and he knew he had made it to the canyon rim. With his last strength he hauled himself over it and lay there panting.

He saw them then—two females. But he saw nothing womanly about them. The lust in their eyes was a lust to kill, and one held a knife and the other a six-gun.

Cimarron looked from one to the other. It was clear that he had a choice—but no chance at all....

Ⓢ SIGNET (0451)

CIMARRON!

- [ ] CIMARRON #3: CIMARRON AND THE BORDER BANDITS
  (122518—$2.50)
- [ ] CIMARRON #4: CIMARRON IN THE CHEROKEE STRIP (123441—$2.50)
- [ ] CIMARRON #5: CIMARRON AND THE ELK SOLDIERS (124898—$2.50)
- [ ] CIMARRON #6: CIMARRON AND THE BOUNTY HUNTERS
  (125703—$2.50)
- [ ] CIMARRON #7: CIMARRON AND THE HIGH RIDER (126866—$2.50)
- [ ] CIMARRON #8: CIMARRON IN NO MAN'S LAND (128230—$2.50)
- [ ] CIMARRON #9: CIMARRON AND THE VIGILANTES (129180—$2.50)
- [ ] CIMARRON #10: CIMARRON AND THE MEDICINE WOLVES
  (130618—$2.50)
- [ ] CIMARRON #11: CIMARRON ON HELL'S HIGHWAY (131657—$2.50)
- [ ] CIMARRON #12: CIMARRON AND THE WAR WOMEN (132521—$2.50)
- [ ] CIMARRON #13: CIMARRON AND THE BOOTLEGGERS (134494—$2.50)
- [ ] CIMARRON #14: CIMARRON ON THE HIGH PLAINS (134850—$2.50)
- [ ] CIMARRON #15: CIMARRON AND THE PROPHET'S PEOPLE
  (135733—$2.50)
- [ ] CIMARRON #16: CIMARRON AND THE SCALP HUNTERS (136659—$2.75)
- [ ] CIMARRON #17: CIMARRON AND THE COMANCHEROS (138120—$2.75)
- [ ] CIMARRON #18: CIMARRON AND THE GUNHAWKS' GOLD (139208—$2.75)

Prices slightly higher in Canada

Buy them at your local bookstore or use this convenient coupon for ordering.

NEW AMERICAN LIBRARY,
P.O. Box 999, Bergenfield, New Jersey 07621

Please send me the books I have checked above. I am enclosing $_____
(please add $1.00 to this order to cover postage and handling). Send check
or money order—no cash or C.O.D.'s. Prices and numbers are subject to change
without notice.

Name_____

Address_____

City_____ State_____ Zip Code_____

Allow 4-6 weeks for delivery.
This offer is subject to withdrawal without notice.

CIMARRON 21
AND THE MANHUNTERS

by
LEO P. KELLEY

A SIGNET BOOK
NEW AMERICAN LIBRARY

PUBLISHER'S NOTE

This novel is a work of fiction. Names, characters, places, and incidents either are the product of the author's imagination or are used fictitiously, and any resemblance to actual persons, living or dead, or events, is entirely coincidental.

NAL BOOKS ARE AVAILABLE AT QUANTITY DISCOUNTS WHEN USED TO PROMOTE PRODUCTS OR SERVICES. FOR INFORMATION PLEASE WRITE TO PREMIUM MARKETING DIVISION, NEW AMERICAN LIBRARY, 1633 BROADWAY, NEW YORK, NEW YORK 10019.

Copyright © 1986 by Leo P. Kelley

All rights reserved

The first chapter of this book previously appeared in *Cimarron and the Red Earth People*, the twentieth volume in this series.

SIGNET TRADEMARK REG. U.S. PAT. OFF. AND FOREIGN COUNTRIES
REGISTERED TRADEMARK—MARCA REGISTRADA
HECHO EN CHICAGO, U.S.A.

SIGNET, SIGNET CLASSIC, MENTOR, PLUME, MERIDIAN AND NAL BOOKS are published by New American Library,
1633 Broadway, New York, New York 10019

First Printing, May, 1986

1 2 3 4 5 6 7 8 9

PRINTED IN THE UNITED STATES OF AMERICA

CIMARRON...

... he was a man with a past he wanted to forget and a future uncertain at best and dangerous at worst. Men feared and secretly admired him. Women desired him. He roamed the Indian Territory with a Winchester '73 in his saddle scabbard, an Army Colt in his hip holster, and a bronc he had broken beneath him. He packed his guns loose, rode his horse hard, and no one dared throw gravel in his boots. Once he had an ordinary name like other men. But a tragic killing forced him to abandon it and he became known only as Cimarron. *Cimarron*, in Spanish, meant wild and unruly. It suited him. *Cimarron*.

1

Cimarron rode up to the small frame house on the eastern side of the Katy railroad's tracks and drew rein. He hallooed the house and a man came out of it to stand staring suspiciously at him. He dug down into a pocket of his jeans and came up with a nickel star that he displayed. "Name's Cimarron," he told the man. "Asked around in town and folks said you could be found out here. I've come about Bob Tucker."

"How much'll you pay me?"

"Ten dollars."

"There's a *fifty*-dollar bounty on Bob Tucker's head so how come you're offering me a measly ten dollars?"

"On account of that's what it's worth to the law—to me—to find out where Bob Tucker's at. The fifty-dollar bounty, that's to be paid to the man who can bring Tucker in, which I reckon isn't you and may be me if I don't happen to get my head blowed off by a back-shooter like Tucker."

"I don't rightly know if I should tell you what I know for just ten dollars," the man whined, shifting his weight from one foot to the other and his chaw from one cheek to the other.

"Mister, when I stopped at the sheriff's office back in McAlester I was told about you and that you were itching to sell some information on the whereabouts of Bob Tucker and—"

"Only to a federal starpacker, though," the man interrupted. "They're the only kind with any money to spend these days, it seems. That sheriff in McAlester wouldn't—claimed he couldn't—pay me a dime for what I know."

"—here I am," Cimarron concluded, ignoring what the man had just said. "Now, I don't like wildgoose chases one little bit. When I find out I'm on one, well, what I generally tend to do is grab the goose I've been chasing and wring its neck. Do you follow me, mister?"

The man nodded. He swallowed. His right hand rose and his fingers encircled his scrawny neck. "The Faber farm," he croaked.

"That's where I'll find Tucker?"

"He's been working there ever since last month when he drifted through these parts. I recognized him right off when I was out to Faber's one day to buy some turnips. I have a pretty good memory for the faces I see printed on dodgers. Once I see such a face, I don't as a rule forget it. It's Tucker for sure." The man held up a hand to Cimarron, who pulled an eagle from his pocket and handed it to him. "Where's the Faber farm?" he asked. When he had been given directions to it, he turned his black and rode away from the house, leaving the man busily biting the gold coin to make sure it wasn't counterfeit.

Later, as Cimarron crested a hill and drew rein, he sat his saddle and stared down at the fields below. Corn shocks stood withering under the thin November sun, and the orchards were bare of fruit and leaves. Beyond the orchard stood a two-story house and outbuilding. Some men were cutting wood and piling it in the bed of a spring wagon. They were too far away for Cimarron to make out their faces, so he couldn't be sure if Bob Tucker was among them.

He put heels to his horse and started down the hill toward the farmhouse. When he reached it, he hallooed it and then gave the grizzled man who emerged from it a cheerful "Good day."

"What can I do for you, stranger?" the man asked.

8

"Are you Mr. Faber who owns this farm?"

"I am. How come you know my name?"

"I asked around in town about where I might find me some work," Cimarron lied. "Somebody mentioned you and your place, so here I am, Mr. Faber, ready and willing to work at anything you want done."

"Folks in town talk without knowing what they're talking about more than half the time," Faber grumbled. "I'm in no need of any hands. Got a bunch of them. Besides, winter's a-coming on and those hands I've got, half of 'em I'll be letting go before the first snow flies."

Cimarron let the disappointment he was feeling show on his face. He wondered if he had failed in his mission before he had barely begun it. If he couldn't hire on here at the Faber farm, he knew, he had no other way of getting close to Bob Tucker. And if he couldn't get close to Tucker, there was no way in the world that he could hope to get evidence to prove that Tucker had murdered Lucy Brandt as he was suspected of having done. And without such evidence, Tucker would probably never be convicted of the crime.

"You say you want work," Faber mused, stroking his bearded chin.

"I'll do whatever needs doing," Cimarron volunteered quickly. "Haul manure, slop hogs—"

"You need work, I take it?"

"And the money it'll put in my empty pockets, yep, I surely do."

"Some of the boys I've hired are about as useless as tits on a boar hog," Faber grunted. "So I'll tell you what I'll do. I'll hire you at half the going rate since I'm doing you a favor taking you on at all this late in the season. Fifty cents a day. Is that agreeable to you?"

"It sure is, Mr. Faber," Cimarron declared enthusiastically, thinking, You old skinflint.

"Then ride on out there to where those boys are working and give them a hand."

Cimarron turned his black and went galloping away toward the cluster of woodcutters in the distance. When he reached them, he dismounted and asked who was in charge of the crew.

"Me," said a burly man. "What business have you here, mister?"

"I was just hired by Mr. Faber to lend you boys a hand."

"Then you'd best get cracking," advised the man in charge as he handed Cimarron an ax. "Start splitting wood."

Cimarron took the ax and approached his quarry, whom he recognized from having seen his picture on dodgers. The man was using a bucking saw to cut up felled trees. "Howdy," he said to Bob Tucker as he placed a piece of wood on a chopping block and split it in two with his ax. "My name's ..." He hesitated, thinking that an owlhoot like Tucker just might be familiar with his name. "It's Smith. Ed Smith."

"Mine's Tom Fenway," Tucker answered without looking at Cimarron, who had to suppress a smile as he thought that Tucker was every bit as good a liar as he was himself.

"Glad to know you, Tom."

No response from Tucker.

Cimarron worked on in silence for a while. When sweat began to stream down his face, he wiped it away and commented, "This kind of work's sure to bust a man's back before long. I wish I were back dealing three-card monte on some fancy Mississippi sternwheeler." He didn't miss the appraising glance Tucker gave him, but his deliberately provocative remark aroused no comment.

Later, the woodcutters made their nooning on food that had been brought from the farmhouse on a flatbed wagon. Cimarron, when he had filled his plate with boiled beans, sourdough biscuits, and a hearty portion of a thick beef and rice stew, made his way to where Tucker was seated alone beneath a blackjack oak. "Mind if I join you, Tom?" he asked, using the assumed name Tucker had given him earlier.

"Suit yourself."

Cimarron sat down next to Tucker. "Grub's real good. Is it always or is this meal an accident?"

"It's passable most days. I've had better—and worse."

"You a logger by trade, Tom?"

"At the moment I am, yes."

Cimarron sopped up some of the stew's broth with a biscuit, which he devoured. He sighed mournfully. "Where'd you work before here, Tom?"

"You sure do ask a man a whole lot of personal questions."

"No offense meant. Didn't mean to pry into your personal business. Meant to find a way to make the time pass easy between us."

Tucker remained silent for a moment and then, apparently mollified, "I've seen better days, as I take it so have you from what you said before about being a riverboat gambler."

"I played my last ace on those old riverboats some time back," Cimarron commented with a wistful note in his voice. "There were some who said I cheated, and try as I might, I couldn't clean the mud off my reputation that some men kept flinging at me."

"You didn't cheat?"

Cimarron gave Tucker a sly grin. "Well, maybe I did use a card pricker from time to time." He shrugged. "So maybe those old boys were right in running me off the river. But I took it all in stride. What the hell else could I do? I mean, if a man gets his ass skinned, all he can do is sit on the blister, right?"

Tucker smiled, put down his empty plate, and pulled the makings from his shirt pocket. He offered them to Cimarron.

"I don't smoke. That's one vice I never took to. Just about the only one, I reckon."

"Let's go, boys!" yelled the man in charge of the woodcutters.

The afternoon passed slowly for Cimarron. He continued to chop wood, which another man piled in the bed of the spring wagon.

"What's Faber fixing to do with all this wood he's put

us to chopping?" Cimarron asked. "He's got himself enough to keep the fires of hell stoked for a good long time by the looks of it."

"He sells it," a man working beside Cimarron answered. "Hear he gets a good price for it too. A lot of the land around here's not timbered and so folks are sorely in need of fuel, come winter. Faber supplies it to them."

"Faber, he must be a mighty rich man to have him as fine a spread as this one," Cimarron commented idly.

"I reckon he does all right," the man who had spoken earlier speculated.

"I never had much of a way with money," Cimarron remarked as he continued chopping wood. "It came and it went and it never stayed around long enough for me to really make its acquaintance. I don't understand for the life of me how men like Faber do it—get rich, I mean."

"By taking advantage of other folks," Tucker interjected, furiously working the bucking saw he had in his hand. "By buying cheap and selling dear," he growled. "It's not fair, if you ask me, for some men to have so much and others so little."

Which leads, Cimarron thought, to a man turning into a rider of the long trails like you, Tucker. But he said nothing more.

That night after supper Cimarron lay on his bunk and watched Tucker shave in front of a cracked mirror nailed to a wooden roof support. Tucker wiped the lather from his face, took off his shirt, washed his face and upper torso, and then put his shirt back on.

"What for are you duding up, Tom?" called out one of the men in the bunkhouse as he winked at the others.

When Tucker made no reply, one of the other men said, "You're wasting your time, Tom, if you think a homely hombre such as yourself can hope to turn the heads of the whores in McAlester."

Still Tucker said nothing, and after a few more taunts

from the men in the bunkhouse, he headed for the door.

Cimarron got up from his bunk, grabbed his hat, and followed Tucker outside. He noted the man was not carrying a gun. "Where are you headed, if you don't mind my asking?"

"Those bastards!" Tucker muttered without answering Cimarron's question. "I may not be Beau Brummell but I wish to hell they'd keep their mouths shut about the way I look."

"Don't let their joshing get to you," Cimarron advised. "It's not always what a man looks like that lets him ram his stopper into one jug after another. It's more a matter of can he sweet-talk a woman and get her as hot as a hen trying to lay a goose egg."

"You're right on that score," Tucker declared enthusiastically. "And this old stopper of mine's plugged more jugs than those old boys in there have probably ever seen!"

"I guess you wouldn't be wanting any company tonight, would you?"

Tucker clapped Cimarron on the shoulder. "You're welcome to ride into town with me if you want to."

"I do want to, on account of I'm about as horny as a six-pointed buck. I washed up before supper, so let's go."

As the two men made their way toward the barn, Cimarron asked, "Where exactly are we going?"

"South McAlester," Tucker answered as they entered the barn and proceeded to get their horses ready to ride.

"You're heading for that part of town folks call Chippy Hill, is that it?"

"That's it," Tucker said as he climbed into his saddle. "With a little bit of luck and an expenditure of a few dollars, both of us are likely to have something a lot sweeter than a sweaty old horse between our legs before this night's over."

* * *

"Want another one, gents?" asked the bar dog in the illegal saloon that was discreetly situated behind a tin shop in the heart of South McAlester.

"Fill 'em up," Tucker directed, and the bar dog promptly filled both glasses.

"To success," Tucker said, raising his glass to Cimarron's.

"To success."

Their glasses touched and then both men drank. Before they could put their glasses back down on the bar, two women sauntered through the batwings and into the saloon, where they paused only briefly before exchanging knowing glances and then heading directly toward Cimarron and Tucker.

" 'Evening, ladies," Cimarron greeted the two women as they arrived at the bar. "Won't you join us?"

"And have something to drink?" Tucker added. "Me and my friend here, we sure could use the sight of some feminine pulchritude such as you both have to offer."

Cimarron and Tucker made room for the two women and summoned the bar dog. When two beers and a bowl of raw oysters had been placed in front of the women, Cimarron handed the bar dog a dollar.

"I'm Ella," announced the blond woman with a saucy toss of her sausage curls, "and this here's my friend, Ida."

The auburn-haired and chestnut-eyed Ida giggled and took a dainty sip from her glass. She patted her full lips with the back of her hand and said, "Ella and me have rooms in the hotel right next door."

"Are you fellows looking for a little fun?" inquired Ella with a coy lifting of her plucked eyebrows.

"You just bet we are," Cimarron replied, "and you two look like you're both chock full of fun."

"What kind of fun did you have in mind?" simpered Ida.

"A quickie or an all-nighter?" Ella asked bluntly.

Cimarron glanced at Tucker, who said, "I've got me

some serious drinking to do, so I'll put my money on a quickie."

"What about you, mister?" Ella asked, batting her eyelashes at Cimarron.

"I reckon I'll have the same as my friend here. How much?"

"Two dollars—each," Ida said.

"Two dollars!" Tucker exploded. "Why, a man can buy the selfsame thing in almost any parlor house here on Chippy Hill for anywhere from four bits to a dollar."

"You're welcome to go to one of those houses, I'm sure," said Ida, quickly downing her beer, "and see if we care. Come along, Ella."

"We're independents," Ella explained as Ida grabbed her arm and tried to pull her away from the bar. "We have to charge a higher price than most of the other whores in the houses around here. We have our hotel rooms to pay for and—"

Cimarron chucked her under the chin, silencing her. "Why, sure you do, honey. I understand. Let's you and me go to your place."

"What about me?" wailed Ida as Cimarron began to guide Ella toward the batwings.

"Come on," Tucker said, and grumbling all the way about Ida's price, he followed Cimarron and Ella out of the saloon with Ida walking haughtily beside him.

They made their way into the lobby of the hotel next door and up the stairs to the second floor, where the women led Cimarron and Tucker down a dreary hall. They stopped at the end of it and Ella announced, "This here's my room," and Ida said, "Mine's the one right next door."

Ella unlocked her door, and then, taking Cimarron's arm, she led him into her room and closed the door behind her. She held out her hand to him. He came up with two dollars, which he gave her and which she tucked between her breasts.

"I don't get undressed for quickies," she informed him. "Neither do you," she added, and flopped down on her back on the bed.

15

"That wasn't what I had in mind."

Ella propped herself up on her elbows and stared at Cimarron. "What wasn't what you had in mind?"

He told her what he had in mind.

"Why not?" was her professional response. She got up from the bed and approached him. "Why don't you have a seat—take a load off your legs?"

He sat down in the only chair in the room and Ella dropped to her knees before him. She unbuttoned his fly, thrust a hand into his jeans, and came up with his already stiff shaft, which she proceeded to stroke, eliciting a contented sigh from Cimarron. She lowered her head, the tip of her tongue protruding from her mouth.

Cimarron, his hands resting on the arms of his chair, watched her tongue snake out to touch his swollen flesh. He spread his legs wide as Ella's tongue teased and tickled him. He was about to order her to get on with it before he exploded, but before he could do so, she opened her mouth wide, lowered her head, and engulfed him. He laid his head against the back of the chair, closed his eyes, and listened to the wet gurgling sounds Ella was making. As her hot tongue skillfully laved him, he tightened his grip on the arms of the chair.

Then he opened his eyes, raised his head, and looked down at her. Her cheeks were drawn in and her lips were tightly pursed around him as her head bobbed up and down in a wildly arousing rhythm. He felt himself growing hotter, felt his face flushing, felt the tingling in his groin as Ella continued using her lips and tongue on him. A kind of giddiness almost overcame him as he felt the sudden surging within him. He moaned. He thrust upward, causing Ella to gag. But she quickly recovered and began to fondle his testicles as her lips continued to grip him.

He couldn't help it; he cried out as he erupted. At first, as he began to flood Ella's mouth, he stiffened; then, with each successive upward thrust and hot spurt, he began to relax until finally, completely spent and totally satisfied, he lay limply back in the chair and stared up at the ceiling without really seeing it.

Ella released him and sat back on her heels. She swallowed, licked her lips, and said, "I thought I was going to choke to death when you rammed it down my throat."

"I got carried away, honey. Didn't mean to cause you any trouble."

Ella smiled. She reached out and playfully pinched Cimarron's still-erect shaft. "I bet this thing has caused more than one girl more trouble than she could handle. Am I right?"

"I always try to look on the bright side of things," he responded with a grin. "I've been told by more than one woman that that thing of mine gave them nothing but pure pleasure."

"I can believe it," Ella said, and got up.

Cimarron stuffed his softening flesh back into his jeans, buttoned up, and got to his feet. Ella threw her arms around him, her hands running up and down his back, caressing his hips, groping between his legs. He stood there enjoying her attentions, as she continued her stroking and provocative petting of his body.

Then, stepping back, she said, "Well, it's time I was getting back to work."

Once outside the room, Cimarron knocked on the door of Ida's room. When he got no response, he called out, "Tom, you in there?"

Still no response.

He made his way down the hall with Ella and together they returned to the saloon, where they found Ida and Tucker drinking at the bar.

"I feel like I could lick my weight in ants," Tucker glumly declared as he and Ida were joined by Cimarron and Ella. "Now the only thing left to do to round off the night is to get drunk," he announced, and emptied his glass.

"What'll you have, another beer?" Cimarron asked Ella.

"Thanks, but no thanks," she answered, shaking her

head, her eyes on two dandified men who had just come into the saloon. "Ida," she muttered, prodding her friend in the ribs with her elbow and pointing at the two men.

Ida turned, saw the two newcomers, and stared toward them with a whispered "Let's go, Ella. There stands four dollars on the hoof."

Tucker didn't turn around as the two women left. "She was as loose as a stretched sheep bladder," he complained. "I kept sliding right out of her."

"Women," Cimarron muttered. "You can't do with them and you can't do without them." He ordered a drink. "They're more trouble than they're worth, take it from me."

Tucker ignored him.

"I could tell you some hair-raising stories," he whispered conspiratorially. "Some of them not so pretty. I swear off the weaker sex from time to time. They're nothing but trouble, every last one of them. A man does well to steer clear of them if he knows what's good for him."

"I've had my share of troubles with women," Tucker mused. He ordered another drink as he watched Ella and Ida leave the saloon with the two dandies.

Cimarron waited for him to go on, hoping Tucker would say something about Lucy Brandt, the woman he was suspected of having murdered, but Tucker slipped into a morose silence.

Two hours and an uncounted number of drinks later, Cimarron's head was still clear because he had secretly spilled most of his drinks into the spittoon that sat on the sawdust-covered floor beside him. He desperately searched his mind for some scheme that would cause Tucker to incriminate himself. Finally he hit on one he thought had a chance of working. After feigning drunkenness for some time, he suddenly began to sob. He lowered his head until it was resting on his crossed forearms, which he had placed on the bar.

"Whatsh the matter?" Tucker asked him in a slurred voice.

"Leave me be." Cimarron shook off the heavy hand Tucker had dropped on his shoulder. "There's no comforting a man like me, who's spilled the blood of a woman, never mind the fact that she was a conniving no-good bitch who had the claws of more men in her flanks than Hannibal ever had in his army.

"She said she was carrying my kid. She said I had to do right by her and marry her. Well, hell, I told her there was no way I would ever do a damn-fool thing like that. She said she'd tell everybody in town what I did to her, get her pa to shoot me." He sobbed again.

"You killed her?"

"Shot her, sure. You don't know what it's like to have killed a woman, my friend. It's not the same as killing a man. It's—"

"I know."

Cimarron shifted position slightly and beckoned to the bar dog, hoping Tucker had not seen him do so. "How many women have you killed?" he asked Tucker, raising his head and throwing one comradely arm around Tucker's shoulder.

"Just one. Her name was Lucy Brandt." Tucker hiccupped. "What you've got to do is you've got to put it clean out of your mind. That's what I did."

"How'd you kill this Lucy Brandt?" Cimarron asked, aware of the gaping and openmouthed bar dog, who was standing stock-still as he listened to the conversation taking place between Cimarron and Tucker. He motioned to the man to be silent.

"Drowned her," Tucker answered. "She was a tease, Lucy Brandt was. All talk and no delivery of the goods. I tried to make it look like she committed suicide, but the law's on my tail anyway."

Cimarron turned to the bar dog. "You heard what he said?"

"I heard him say he drowned to death a woman named Lucy Brandt." The bar dog's face was white.

Cimarron pulled his badge from his pocket and showed it to Tucker, causing the man to take several staggering steps away from him and the bar dog to blink several times in rapid succession. "I'm a deputy marshal," he told the bar dog. "This man here is named Bob Tucker and he's wanted, like he said, for the murder of Lucy Brandt. I needed evidence against him that would stand up in court and I got it—his confession, which you heard. What's your name?"

"Edward Peters. Why?"

"There'll be a deputy who'll come to collect you. You'll be needed as a prosecution witness against Tucker at his trial since you heard his confession the same as me."

"You—" Tucker gripped the edge of the bar to keep from falling as he swayed drunkenly in front of Cimarron. "You won't take me!"

Cimarron calmly watched Tucker weave his unsteady way toward the batwings. He watched him fall to the floor before he reached them. He went to Tucker and helped him to his feet. "Let's go, Tucker. You and me are heading for Fort Smith."

But Tucker never heard him, Cimarron realized, because the man had passed out. He tossed Tucker's limp body over his shoulder and started for the batwings.

"Wait a minute, Deputy," the bar dog called out. "You and your friend haven't settled your bar bill."

Cimarron turned around. "How much is owing you?"

"Six bits."

Cimarron thrust a hand into his pocket—and swore when he realized that all his money was gone. Ella, he thought. When she was feeling me all over just before we left her room—she wasn't just being affectionate like I thought at the time. She was stealing my poke.

He went back to the bar, retrieved a five-dollar bill he kept hidden in his left boot, and handed it to the bar dog. When he received his change, he left the bar. Outside, he looked up at the hotel's second floor. I can't leave Tucker unattended, he thought, which means I don't get to go after my stolen money. So Ella wins the game and gets to keep what she stole from me. Well, at least I've got Tucker, which was what I set out to do, and he's worth two dollars to me when I turn him in. He draped Tucker over the man's saddle. Then, leading Tucker's horse, he rode out of town.

As they neared the Katy depot, Tucker groaned. Cimarron looked back over his shoulder and then drew rein. "Get into that saddle of yours," he ordered Tucker, his words almost drowned out by the shriek of a Katy train that was just starting to pull out.

Tucker, after getting aboard his horse, gave Cimarron a glare before riding out.

The two men rode without speaking as the train on their left began to gather speed, its wheels screeching and its whistle screaming. The lamp on the locomotive sent a bright beam of light into the darkness beyond the depot, but it came nowhere near Cimarron and his prisoner.

Tucker began to wave his arms and point at his horse, but the noise of the train prevented Cimarron from hearing what he was saying.

Cimarron rode up beside him and finally understood that Tucker was trying to tell him that his cinch had worked loose. Cimarron indicated with a nod and a blunt gesture that Tucker could dismount and tighten it. He sat his saddle as Tucker dismounted and bent down to peer under his horse's barrel. Then, in one swift move, Tucker ducked under his horse, came up on the other side of the animal and went running toward the train.

"Tucker, stop!" Cimarron roared, doubting that he could be heard above the roar and iron rattle of the train.

Tucker continued running rapidly in the direction of the train, which was showering the area with cinders from its smokestack.

Cimarron heeled his black and rounded Tucker's mount as he set out after his fleeing prisoner. When Tucker increased his speed, Cimarron fired a high and wide warning shot; Tucker kept on running, his arms stretched out in front of him.

The train climbed a low grade and simultaneously began to round a bend as Cimarron, still galloping in pursuit of Tucker, fired another warning shot at the man. This time his shot struck Tucker because the man had suddenly veered sharply to one side in a desperate attempt to leap aboard the train's caboose. Tucker stumbled. And then he ran on for a few more steps. His outstretched hands clawed at the air. He let out a loud wail and went down. He rose to his knees and reached out as if to embrace the caboose that was rapidly vanishing around the bend. He fell again and this time he did not rise.

When Cimarron reached Tucker a moment later, he dismounted and hunkered down beside him. He placed two fingers against the man's neck, and when he felt no pulse, he swore.

He stood up, thinking that the night had been a bad one. And not just for Tucker. For him as well. Ella had stolen his money. And now he had, without intending to, shot and killed his prisoner, which meant two unpleasant things: one, he would have to pay, as was required by law, for the man's burial; two, he would not get to collect the two dollars due him for bringing Tucker to the jail in Fort Smith. Two dollars wasn't all that much, he thought, but it sure was better than nothing.

As Cimarron was passing through Poteau in Choctaw Nation the next day, he was wondering how he was going to explain to Marshal Upham, once he reached Fort Smith, that he was in desperate need of a cash advance against future earnings. Upham, he was certain, would rant and rave and accuse him of being impecunious just as he had done on several other similar occasions. The last thing I need, he thought, is a holier-than-thou lecture on how to manage my money from the righteous likes of Marshal Daniel P. Upham. But somehow or other, I've got to wheedle some cash money out of the marshal, else I'll be going hungry and trail-dirty since I can't at the moment buy me so much as a corn muffin or a barbershop bath. That undertaker in McAlester relieved me of my last cent and still insisted he was losing money on Tucker's burial.

Cimarron's train of thought was derailed as he heard the shouting and saw the two men going at it knuckle and skull in the dust they were raising in the middle of the street just ahead. He was about to ride by them when a way of solving his financial problem suddenly occurred to him.

He drew rein and stared thoughtfully at the two men who were busily battering each other to the delight of the growing crowd that surrounded them. One of the pair had a bloody nose. The other had a split lower lip. Both had numerous facial bruises and bloody knuckles. Cimarron got out of the saddle and wrapped his reins around a nearby hitchrail. He rooted about in his pockets until he came up with a piece of paper and the stub of a pencil. Wetting the pencil's lead point, he asked the man standing next to him for his name.

"What do you want my name for?"

"You're a witness," Cimarron replied, "and I'm a deputy marshal."

"That still don't tell me what for you want my name."

"You saw that fellow"—Cimarron pointed at one of the fighting men—"try to kill that other fellow, and the other fellow try to do the selfsame thing to the first fellow, which is, in my book, the crime of attempted murder. You'll have to come to Fort Smith with me and give your eyewitness testimony when those two jaspers go on trial."

"They're not trying to kill each other," the man protested. "They're just fighting nice and natural."

"That's not the way I see it, and I've got the eyes of an eagle when it comes to uncovering crimes. Now, your name . . ."

The man began to back away from Cimarron.

"Stand hitched," Cimarron ordered him. "If you don't give me your name, I'll have to arrest you for obstructing justice and you'll wind up in jail right alongside those two would-be murderers there."

Reluctantly the man gave his name and Cimarron

wrote it down. He moved on to another man and repeated the process. By the time he was finished, he had the names of nineteen witnesses to what he declared were the crimes of attempted murder.

At fifty cents a head, he calculated, that means I can collect nine dollars and fifty cents for these witnesses plus six cents a mile one way between here and Fort Smith, which'll bring me another four dollars or thereabouts. Though it sure won't make me rich, that money'll keep me from being the pauper I am at present.

He drew his gun and yelled, "Hold it, gents!"

He had to yell his order a second time before the two bare-knuckled warriors paid him any attention. "You two are under arrest," he told both badly battered men, "and you're coming with me. You—what's your name?"

The man Cimarron had questioned answered, "Dawes. But what—"

"What's your name?" Cimarron asked the other man.

"Randall. Who the hell are you?"

"I'm a deputy marshal here in Indian Territory. Randall, you and Dawes are both under arrest for attempting to murder each other. I'm taking both of you to Fort Smith to stand trial on that charge along with these nineteen witnesses to your crimes that I've just rounded up."

Cimarron knocked on the door of Marshal Upham's office, and when the marshal's gruff voice yelled, "Come in," he shepherded Dawes and Randall into the office.

"Well, now, what have we here?" Upham inquired as he sat back in his chair.

"Collared these two jaspers over in Poteau in Choctaw Nation, Marshal," Cimarron answered. "You can put them down on Judge Parker's docket as attempted murderers."

"Who did they try to kill?"

"Each other, that's who. I saw what happened and I'll testify at their trial if you need me to. But you most likely won't be needing me, seeing as how I've brought to town nineteen witnesses to the crimes." Cimarron pulled his list of witnesses' names from his pocket and tossed it on the desk. "I brought them all with me so they could participate in the trial of these two would-be assassins."

"Marshal," Dawes ventured with a wary glance in Cimarron's direction, "there's not a word of truth to what this deputy said."

"We weren't trying to kill each other, Marshal," Randall stated meekly. "We were just having a bit of a disagreement."

"Which we were in the act of settling when this deputy appeared on the scene and arrested us," Dawes declared indignantly.

Upham gave Cimarron a baleful glance.

But before he could say anything, Cimarron said, "Marshal, I'll just take the nine-fifty that's due me for bringing in those nineteen witnesses I told you about and the six cents a mile between here and Poteau that's also due me."

"Hold on one minute," Upham said. Turning to Dawes and Randall, he asked, "What weapons were you boys using on each other?"

"None Marshal," Dawes replied.

"Only our fists, Marshal," Randall amended.

"Fists can be deadly weapons," Cimarron quickly pointed out. "Now, about the fees that are due me, Marshal—"

Upham held up a hand for silence. Then, summoning his clerk from an adjoining office, he handed the man the list of names that Cimarron had tossed on the desk. "Check the hotels and the saloons," he instructed the clerk. "Bring in as many of these nineteen men as you can find. I want to hear their side of this story. And make it snappy. I want you back here inside of twenty minutes."

"Marshal," Cimarron began when the clerk had departed, "I'm insulted."

"Are you now? Why, pray tell?"

"I am on account of you don't seem to be putting any credence into what I just told you about these two evildoers standing before me. Why, one or both of them might be dead right this very minute if I didn't—at great risk to my own safety and well-being, I'll have you know—stop them from killing each other."

Upham merely harrumphed.

"Why don't you just pay me what's due me, Marshal, and I'll be moseying along."

No response from Upham.

Cimarron was still trying to persuade Upham to pay him what he was owed when the clerk returned with three men and announced that they were the only witnesses he could locate in the short time that had been alloted to him.

Upham proceeded to question them.

"Randall and Dawes here," drawled one of the three men, "they fight at the drop of a hat, so it ain't nothing to take so serious."

"Whenever these two meet up with each other," volunteered a second man, "they take to fightin' even before the howdies is over."

"They wouldn't try to kill each other," offered the third man, "cuz if'n they did, they wouldn't have any chance to fight each other anymore, not with one of them dead."

Dawes grinned.

Randall guffawed.

Upham glared at Cimarron.

Cimarron tried and failed to think of anything to say.

"You gentlemen are free to go," Upham told Dawes, Randall, and the three witnesses.

Cimarron started to follow them out the door.

"You, Deputy, are *not* free to go," Upham bellowed. "Come back here!

"That was the most obviously trumped-up case I've seen since I've been in this office and, believe me, I've seen a few such cases before," Upham thundered when Cimarron was again standing in front of his desk. "I don't know what made you think you could get away with it. And all for a matter of a few dollars in mileage and witness fees."

Cimarron suddenly exploded. "So you don't know why I did it, don't you? Well, I'll tell you why I did it!"

"Aha! Then you admit you trumped up this case."

"You're damn right I admit it. And why did I do it? For money, that's why."

"The root of all evil."

"If money's the root of all evil, as some folks claim it is, then I must be close to becoming a saint since I always seem to have so little of it."

"Cimarron, I am ashamed of you and what you just did. Not only did you disrupt the lives of twenty-one people, albeit temporarily, but you also risked damage to the reputation of this office and Judge Parker's court. You—"

"I don't want to hear any pious preacher talk from you, Marshal," Cimarron warned, anger rioting through him now. "Not when I haven't got so much as two cents to rub against one another. Not when I'm in need of a meal I can't pay for. Not when my saddle needs repair and I can't pay to have it fixed. Not when you pay your deputies next to nothing and they have to stoop to stunts like the one I just tried pulling on you to get their hands on enough cash to keep body and soul together."

"I know the fees we pay you deputies are low, Cimarron," Upham said sternly. "But that is no reason to risk dishonoring the judicial process and your own integrity as an officer of this court."

Cimarron leaned over the desk. "Marshal, I've been shot at—and hit—a whole lot of times in the performance of my duty out there west of hell's fringe in what polite people call Indian Territory. I've had horses shot out from under me. I've been tormented and tortured in more ways than I care to count by villains and miscreants I was after. Sometimes I think I must be crazy to keep at it day in and day out. And now when I hear you lecturing me about how to behave— and all because I need to earn a decent wage—well, no more, Marshal. This right here and now is it. I'm through. Finished. You can hire yourself somebody else to take my place. Somebody dim-witted and foolhardy enough to want to die out there in the Territory for no good reason that anybody anywhere can think of."

Cimarron pulled his badge from his pocket and threw it on the desk. Then he turned on his heels and started for the door.

"Wait a minute, Cimarron. Let's be reasonable men about this. Let's talk it over. I'm sure we can work something out."

But Marshal Upham's words didn't stop Cimarron, who stormed out of the office. Once outside, he halted on the courthouse steps. What do I do now? he asked himself.

He could think of no answer to his question.

2

Cimarron made his way down the courthouse steps and then headed for the opening in the stone wall that surrounded the compound containing the courthouse and gallows. As he emerged on Garrison Street, he almost collided with Charley Burns, who was in charge of the jail, which was located in the basement of the courthouse.

"Well, hello there, and how the hell are you, Cimarron?" Charley greeted him. "You sure stayed gone a long while this time. Where you been?"

"Out around McAlester, Charley. How've things been with you?"

"Fair to middling, except where that damn jail of mine's concerned. It's as crowded as ever, and life for those unfortunate enough to find themselves in it's rougher than corncobs. And I suppose you've just gone and seen to it that it's even more crowded.

"Nope, Charley, I've not."

"You come to town empty-handed this time, have you?"

Cimarron nodded. "I accidentally shot the jasper I was after, which leaves me without the two dollars I'd've collected had I brought him in with me to Judge Parker's hotel that you keep so well." Cimarron hesitated and then, "Charley, you could do me a real big favor should you be willing."

Charley clucked to himself and thrust a hand into his pocket. He came up with a small leather purse, which he snapped open. "How much this time, Cimarron?"

"Could you spare a dollar, Charley? I hate like hell asking you for another loan, but I'm busted and that's a sad fact."

"Don't worry about it. Glad to do it. After all, what are friends for?"

"Well, friends certainly aren't for playing at being a banker, that much is for sure."

"Here," Charley said, and handed Cimarron five dollars instead of the one he had asked for. "Pay me back when you can."

"In all fairness, Charley, I got to warn you that might not be for quite a spell."

"Oh, you'll catch yourself a bunch of bad boys the next time you go on the scout, and then you'll be rolling in money again."

"I won't be going on the scout anymore, Charley."

"You won't be? Why not?"

"I just turned my badge in to Marshal Upham. I've washed my hands of lawdogging once and for all."

Charley's lower jaw dropped. "Why in the world—"

"Would I do a thing like that?"

Charley nodded.

"On account of I just got fed up with the way I've been risking my ass out there in the Territory and not getting anywhere even close to decent pay for doing so."

"That the whole story, is it?" Charley asked suspiciously.

"Sure it is. You don't doubt me, do you?"

"Well, I know what a hot-tempered type of man you are, Cimarron, so naturally I wondered if there might not be a nigger in the wood pile somewhere."

Cimarron shrugged. "On my way back here after I'd killed that fellow without meaning to, I kept turning over in my mind ways I could maybe make myself a dollar or two. I finally came up with the idea of trumping up a case and hauling some witnesses in to court to testify at a trial. But Upham, he caught me out slick as

30

a whistle and began berating me. Never mind that I had to pay to bury the man I shot and never mind that fair's fair. He went at me like some kind of holier-than-thou preacher man trying to get one of the drags to come on up and be saved. Well, sir, I finally had just about all I could take from him, so I told him to take his job and shove it."

Charley sighed. "You are a caution, Cimarron. Can't you learn to smile and swallow what Upham has to dish out once he gets on one of his high horses?"

"Nope. I can't. Won't. Not now, not never."

"Well, I got to admit that you got yourself a point. Sometimes I think a man has to be loco to sign up to ride for Judge Parker. All the job gets a man is low pay, bad company, and the chance to put his life on the line day in and day out."

"That's just exactly what I told Upham. That, and that I'd finally come to my senses. That I was intent on finding myself some sort of sensible kind of job, something that'd let me sleep easy at nights and walk the streets of a town in the Territory without I have to keep looking over my shoulder every step of the way."

"Cimarron, this whole thing's none of my business and I know that, but maybe you'll let me ask you this: why don't you sleep on it? Think it over? I heard Judge Parker's sent some more letters to the politicians back in the States about how they never have appropriated anywheres near enough money to pay you boys what he—and Marshal Upham, too, if the truth's to be told—think you rightfully deserve. Maybe this time those lawmakers'll come through with a new law and deputies like you will start earning some fair fees for the services you perform."

"The judge has tried and tried to squeeze a few dollars out of Congress, as we both know, Charley. Time and time again he has. Only so far he's had no luck at all, as we also both know. Nope, Charley, I've had it. I'm out now and I'm staying out. In fact, I'm moving on.

"Where to?"

31

"I'm damned if I know, to tell you the truth, Charley. That there's a question I just can't answer at the moment. All I can say is that a loose horse is always looking for new pastures, so I reckon I'll find something to occupy my mind and take up my time. It's been good knowing you, Charley, even though you did lodge me in that hell hole of a jail of yours once upon a real unhappy time."

As the two men shook hands, Charley said, "I'll miss you, Cimarron. I hope things work out for you. I hate to see a good man down on his luck."

Cimarron clapped Charley on the back. "I'll get by, one way or the other. I've ridden a rough string most of my life. That tends to toughen a man. Makes him mean and ornery.

"You talk tough all right, I'll grant you that. But I've seen another side of you from time to time. The side that's as soft as a spring rain."

Cimarron shook a playful finger in Charley's face. "Don't you dare tell anybody what you *claim* to have seen."

"Don't take any wooden nickels, Cimarron."

"Be seeing you, Charley." Cimarron strode down Garrison Street on his way to the nearest barbershop. He arranged for a bath, which he took in a tin tub in the back of the shop, and then, when he was dressed again, he sat in one of the two barber chairs in the front of the shop and had his hair shorn and his cheeks and chin shaved. "I look like a new-minted man," he commented as he studied himself in the barber's full-length mirror. "Damned if I don't."

The man Cimarron saw in the mirror was tall—well over six feet—and he was rawboned and rangy. The spare flesh on his slender frame was taut and heavily muscled. He had broad shoulders, a narrow waist, a thick chest, and four long strong limbs. His hands were wide and his fingers large-knuckled and bony. The exposed skin of his face and hands had been sun-bronzed and weather-worn.

Slung low around his hips was a black leather cartridge belt, all of its loops filled. The oiled holster hanging from it was tied down with a rawhide thong that circled his right thigh and it housed his .44 Frontier Colt revolver.

He wore a brown bib shirt that was missing a button under his buckskin jacket, a tan bandanna, jeans faded from many washings, and low-heeled, knee-high black army boots that were streaked with trail dust. The hat he had taken down from a wall peg and clapped on his head was a black flat-topped stetson.

His face was as lean as his body and as firm and unyielding. He had a broad forehead. Eyebrows as black as the straight hair that covered his ears and the nape of his neck. A thin nose with flared nostrils. Eyes like emeralds. Sunken cheeks. Thin lips above a square jaw. A scar began just below his left eye and ran down his cheek to end just above the corner of his mouth.

The man in the mirror had heard himself called handsome by more than one woman, and he had heard himself called ugly names by more men than he cared to count. He grinned at Cimarron, who said to the barber, "I look so brand-new I hardly know myself."

After leaving the barbershop, Cimarron made his way toward the restaurant directly across the street. He circled the hogs that were wallowing in the muddy bog the street had become as a result of a recent rain, and once seated inside the restaurant, he ordered steak, fried eggs, boiled potatoes, and coffee.

When the white-aproned owner of the restaurant set his plate before him, he began to devour the food, forking it eagerly into his mouth and hardly bothering to chew it, so hungry was he. After emptying his plate and finishing the last of his coffee, he got up and paid for his meal. He had just clapped his hat on his head when the sound of a shot caused him to spin around and peer through the restaurant's dusty windows to the street.

When another round was fired, he ran from the restaurant. Outside on the broadwalk, he looked up and down the street, seeking the source of the gunshots; at first he saw only scurrying people hurriedly taking refuge in shops and alleyways. Then, as he caught the glint of sunlight on a rifle barrel out of the corner of his eye, he looked up and saw a man crouching behind the arched top of the false front on a bakery.

His hand dropped to the butt of his Colt as his eyes dropped to the man who had positioned himself behind one of the pillars supporting the overhang in front of the drugstore. He watched the man take aim at the rifleman on the roof opposite him.

Before the man behind the pillar could fire, the rifleman shot the revolver out of his hand. As the disarmed man stiffened, apparently unwilling to leave the scant safety of the pillar to retrieve his six-gun, Cimarron drew his .44 and fired. As he had intended, his shot went over the rifleman's head, causing him to drop down out of sight behind the top of the bakery's false front.

"Get inside!" Cimarron shouted to the disarmed man.

But the man didn't move. "He'll kill me if I try to run for it," he shouted.

Cimarron was about to make a move toward the man, intending to try to get him to a safer position, when the rifleman fired again, this time at Cimarron. He leapt to one side as a bullet bit into the wooden wall of the barbershop behind him. He dropped down behind a wooden water trough and returned the man's fire.

"I'll keep him busy," he shouted to the man still sheltering behind the pillar. "When I start shooting, you make a run for it. Get yourself inside that drugstore."

"My gun—"

"Forget your gun for right now. Get inside where you'll be safe. You ready to run?"

The man swallowed, nodded.

Cimarron quickly thumbed two cartridges from loops on his gun belt and used them to fill the empty chambers of his six-gun. A moment later, he yelled, "Now!" and began firing at the rifleman on the roof of the bakery, driving him down. He was pleased to see the man who had been disarmed make a dash across the broadwalk and dart inside the open door of the drugstore. He looked up, expecting the rifleman to reappear. He waited, his finger tight against the trigger of his gun.

The rifleman did not reappear.

Cimarron hesitated for only a moment. Then he was up and, six-gun still in hand, running across the street, then down the alleyway between the bakery and a dry-goods store. At the far end of the alley, he halted. With his back pressed against the wall of the bakery, he cautiously peered around the corner of the building. No one in sight. He listened but could hear nothing. He eased around the corner, then ran to the far side of the building. He swore when he saw the steps that descended from the second floor along that side of the building, the steps he had not been able to see from his former position behind the water trough.

That gunman got down those stairs, he thought, and by now he's long gone. He must have had a horse somewheres nearby. He was about to holster his Colt, when a woman's scream caused him to tighten his grip on his gun and look up. A door suddenly flew open and the rifleman burst out onto the second-floor landing, while behind him the unseen woman continued to scream.

"Hold it right there," Cimarron shouted as the man with the rifle started down the steps.

Instead of obeying Cimarron's shouted command, the rifleman spun around and fired. When his badly aimed round slammed into the wooden banister, Cimarron ducked back around the corner of the building. He took aim and fired as the man pounded down the steps that led to the street.

He missed.

The rifleman reached the bottom of the steps and disappeared. Cimarron sprang out from where he had taken cover and went racing past the steps on his way toward the street. He had almost reached the front of the building when a horseman appeared directly in front of him and he recognized the rider as the rifleman. Before he could fire, the mounted man sent a bullet plowing through the flesh of Cimarron's left shoulder, half-turning him around by the force of its impact.

Ignoring the pain in his arm and the hot blood that was soaking his flesh and bullet-torn shirt sleeve, Cimarron ran into the street. He could see neither the fleeing rifleman nor the man's mount. He could see only the dust being raised by the horse as it galloped down the empty street, heading east out of town.

Cimarron stood there for a moment, muttering curses under his breath; then he glanced back at the steps. He thought of the woman who was screaming. Holstering his gun, he began to climb the steps. Before he had reached the landing on the second floor, the woman came out upon it, her face pale, her hands clutched together in front of her.

"Is he gone?" she asked Cimarron in a shaky voice.

"He's gone. Did he hurt you?"

"No. He broke in upon me. I thought he was going to kill me. Are you quite sure he's gone?"

Cimarron nodded. "He wanted a place to hide and he picked yours, is that it?"

It was the woman's turn to nod.

"From now on, I suggest you keep your door locked, ma'am."

The woman looked at Cimarron as if he had spoken an obscenity. "I have never had to lock my door. Not here in Fort Smith, which I have always believed was a civilized city—until today. I don't know what this world is coming to!" The woman left the landing and slammed the door behind her.

As he made his way back down the stairs, Cimarron heard a key turning in a lock above him. She acted there at the end like it was my fault what happened, he thought. Like I was the one brought her world to the pretty pass it's reached. He grinned. I'll wager she keeps more than her door locked from now on. She'll keep her windows locked too, or I miss my guess.

He crossed the street and, before entering the drugstore, picked up the gun that lay on the boardwalk. Inside he gave the gun to the man who had been engaged in the gunfight with the rifleman.

He was a short stocky man with light-brown eyes and dark-brown hair. He had long sideburns, full lips that looked as if he had just licked them, and puffy cheeks Cimarron decided the slightly corpulent and indolent looking man might pass for a merchant of some sort Might, but for his eyes, which were cold and piercing. He's got the eyes, Cimarron thought, of a sidewinder.

"Is he gone?" the man asked Cimarron, echoing the woman's question, as he holstered the gun Cimarron had given him.

"He's gone," Cimarron answered. "Now maybe you won't mind telling me what that little fracas was all about?"

The man rose from the crate on which he had been sitting and shook hands with Cimarron. "My name is Sam Murdoch and I want to thank you sincerely for coming to my assistance the way you just did. I appreciate what you did for me. You may very well have saved my life."

"My name's Cimarron."

"Cimarron," the man repeated, his eyes narrowing and his husky voice deepening. "You wouldn't happen to be the same Cimarron who serves Judge Parker's court as a deputy marshal, would you?"

"That's me. You've heard tell of me?"

"Oh, I have indeed. Yes, I have heard quite remarkable tales of you and your prowess in support of law and order. Now, I know that I can believe those tales after having just seen your behavior in my behalf, even though some of the tales I have been told about you and your exploits did, I must frankly say, strain my credulity at the time."

Cimarron let Murdoch's last remark pass. "Who was that man with the rifle and why was he throwing down on you, Murdoch? Or was it you who started slinging lead?"

"Sir," said the clerk behind the counter in a timid voice as he addressed Cimarron, "you're hurt. That wound—it should be seen by a doctor."

"I thank you for your concern," Cimarron told the man. "But it looks a lot worse than it really is on account of the way I've been bleeding like a stuck pig. I'll get me something to wrap around it first chance I get."

"Let me escort you to a doctor," Murdoch suggested in a concerned voice. "I feel it is my duty to do so, since you were wounded while defending me."

"Doctors, Murdoch, cost money and I've got very little. I'll be fine."

"You will be when that wound is tended to," Murdoch persisted. Turning to the clerk, he asked, "Where is the nearest doctor located?"

When he had received directions, he took Cimarron by his uninjured arm and led him out of the drugstore.

Later, in the doctor's office, Murdoch stood by while the doctor sterilized and then stitched Cimarron's wound. When he had bandaged it, Murdoch paid the man's fee and left the office with Cimarron.

"I noticed a dry-goods store across the alley from the bakery," Murdoch commented, and led the way to it.

There, at Murdoch's insistence, Cimarron selected a dark-blue flannel shirt that Murdoch promptly paid for. He put the shirt on and asked the clerk to dispose of his ripped and bloodied one.

Outside, Murdoch pointed down the street. "There's a likely place."

Cimarron stared at the saloon Murdoch had pointed out and then at Murdoch. "I'm obliged to you for what you've done for me, but I reckon I'll have to draw the line where bellying up to a bar's concerned. There's such a thing as taking advantage of a man's good nature—me taking advantage of yours, I mean."

"Nonsense," Murdoch exclaimed jovially, making a dismissive gesture. "It's not charity I'm offering you, Cimarron, although that would be well-warranted under the circumstances. No, call it a down payment of a sort."

"Down payment?" Cimarron asked as he and Murdoch headed for the saloon.

"Perhaps I am being presumptuous," Murdoch stated as they entered the empty saloon and took places at the long mahogany bar directly opposite the bar dog. "But I am hoping that you and I, Cimarron, might be able to make a business arrangement that will prove to be mutually beneficial."

The bar dog made a sound somewhere between a snort and a cough. "Pardon me," he said to Murdoch, "but I couldn't help hearing what you just said. I must say you're one lucky fellow, you are. I saw from the doorway what just happened out there on the street. That man with the rifle might have put you out of business once and for all were it not for this fellow here." The bar dog indicated Cimarron with a blunt gesture.

"That, sir, is a fact I won't dispute," Murdoch agreed. He ordered beer and asked Cimarron what he would have.

Cimarron hesitated, and then, as a result of Murdoch's eager urging, he ordered whiskey.

"You asked me in the drugstore about the identity of the man on the bakery's roof," Murdoch remarked as the bar dog served him and then Cimarron. "You wanted to know why he was shooting at me," he continued as the bar dog listened avidly to his every word. "You wanted to know why he was shooting at me. You wondered, as I recall, which one of us had begun the gun battle. The man who was trying to kill me is named Bill Tolliver, and it was he, not I, who began the fight."

Cimarron raised his glass and downed the whiskey it contained.

"Another," said Murdoch to the hovering bar dog, pointing to Cimarron's empty glass. When it had been filled, he continued, "I hope, Cimarron, that what I am about to tell you will not cause you to find my company unappealing." Murdoch gazed thoughtfully at Cimarron over the rim of his glass for a moment and then drank from it. "Men who are engaged in my profession are not always accorded the warmest of welcomes among many people."

When Murdoch said no more, Cimarron, his curiosity aroused, asked, "What profession are you talking about?"

"I am a bounty hunter, Cimarron."

Cimarron sipped his whiskey.

"Does that disturb you?"

"Nope."

"Perhaps it is just that I am somewhat defensive about the manner in which I earn my living. But I have found to my sorrow that bounty hunters are not always held in the highest regard by quite a number of people, as you may know."

"I know. The selfsame thing holds true in my case. There are folks out in Indian Territory who'd as soon shoot a deputy marshal as give him the time of day. And I'm not talking about hard cases wanted by the law. I'm talking about so-called God-fearing decent citizens. They just don't have much liking for the law and they tend to try their best to thwart men like me who are bent on enforcing it.

"You and me, Murdoch, could be called birds of a feather. We both work for the law. Neither one of us is much loved on account of what we do. But both of us do society a service whether or not society wants to admit that fact to our faces."

"I've had upstanding members of society spit in my face," Murdoch remarked solemnly. And then, brightening, he continued, "I'm glad to know you feel the way you do, Cimarron. It puts my mind to ease. And now I think it is a good time to discuss the business arrangement I mentioned to you earlier."

"You said, as I recollect, that it might do us both some good, this business arrangement you've got in mind, whatever it might turn out to be."

"Yes, indeed, it very well might. What I had in mind was this, Cimarron. I want you to side me on a journey

I am about to make into Indian Territory. I know your reputation as a fearless gunman—"

"Lawman, Murdoch, lawman."

"Lawman, then."

"And not always so fearless a lawman neither. There have been times out in the Territory when I've been scared stone-stiff."

"But I am willing to wager that you nevertheless conducted yourself admirably despite your fear."

"I managed."

"Well, to continue. Bill Tolliver, Cimarron, is the brother of a man named Al Tolliver. Al Tolliver was wanted by the authorities in the state of Arkansas for murdering a bank teller in cold blood while he and his partner, a man named Dusty Atkins, were attempting to rob a bank. I—"

"You tracked Al down, caught him, and turned him over to the law."

"That's correct. I did. But Dusty Atkins, who was also wanted by the law, eluded me. Well, the long and the short of it is that Al Tolliver's brother vowed to kill me for what I did. He has been trailing me ever since the day his brother was hanged—for nearly a week now—but I thought I had given him the slip. Obviously I was wrong. If you hadn't shown up when you did and come to my aid—"

"You probably could have taken Tolliver," Cimarron interrupted.

"Possibly. But after I had escaped into the drugstore with your help, it occurred to me that with you by my side I would have a far better chance of getting through Indian Territory alive than if I attempted the journey on my own with that bloodthirsty Bill Tolliver dogging my heels."

"You think Tolliver will have another try at taking you down?"

"Of course he will. There's not the slightest doubt in my mind about that."

"Where exactly are you headed in Indian Territory?"

"Wetumka in Creek Nation. Do you know the place?"

"I know it. Wetumka's tucked in nice and neat between the Canadian River on the north and Wetumka Creek on the south. I've been there a time or two."

"I'll pay you well to make the journey with me, Cimarron. How does two hundred dollars sound to you?"

"Two hundred dollars sounds just fine to me."

"I'll pay you a hundred before we set out and the other hundred when we reach Wetumka safely."

"Got a question for you, Murdoch."

"Ask it."

"Do you happen to know where Bill Tolliver lives?"

"Yes, I do. He lives about two miles north of Van Buren, Arkansas. He and his late lamented brother worked a farm of some ninety acres there that abutted the farm of their uncle, Obadiah Hoyt, from whom they bought the land a few years ago." Murdoch chuckled. "Bill was the one who did most of the work with the help of a hired hand or two from time to time. Al was off most of the time riding the owlhoot trail. Why do you ask, Cimarron?"

"On account of it crossed my mind that maybe what would be best for me to do instead of riding with you all the way across Creek Nation to Wetumka is I maybe ought to hightail it up to Van Buren and see to it that Bill Tolliver loses his taste for trailing you."

Murdoch was silent for a moment. Then, "I think it would be better if we stuck to my original plan. You may be unsuccessful in locating Tolliver. He may not be at his farm. In fact, he may very well still be stalking me right here and now in Fort Smith. I appreciate your suggestion, Cimarron, but I think I would prefer to have you accompany me to Wetumka."

"You're paying the freight, Murdoch, so we'll do it your way. When do you want to leave?"

Murdoch glanced nervously at the batwings as if he were expecting to see Bill Tolliver come crashing through them, gun in hand. "How about right now? Can you leave immediately, Cimarron, or is that too short a notice for you? I realize you have other obligations, ties here in town—"

Cimarron shook his head. "I'm ready to go right now if you are. We'll need some supplies and a horse to pack them on since towns between here and Wetumka are few and far between."

"You fellows heading for Wetumka?" asked the bar dog, who had been listening with great interest to the conversation of his only two customers. "That town's a terror, I've heard it said."

Cimarron, ignoring the man, asked Murdoch if he had a horse.

"Yes, my buckskin's at the local livery." Murdoch thrust a hand into the inner pocket of his coat and brought out his wallet. He counted out one hundred dollars, which he handed to Cimarron.

Cimarron took the money, pocketed it, and then, when Murdoch had paid for their drinks, both men left the saloon.

3

"I want a horse that leads easy," Cimarron told the man in charge of the livery as he and Murdoch entered the establishment. "I want one that won't chafe under a heavy pack."

"I don't know as I can supply what you want," said the liveryman doubtfully. "I've only got one horse for sale and he's getting on in years. But he might do if you don't treat him too rough. How far do you plan on journeying with him?"

"Down to Wetumka in Creek Nation," Murdoch replied.

"Let's see this animal you've got," Cimarron said, and he and Murdoch followed the stableman into the rear of the livery, where the man pointed to a stalled bay.

Cimarron entered the stall and was pleased to see that the bay did not startle or shy away from him. But he was not pleased to note, as he reached for the animal's mouth to examine its teeth, that the bay began to crib the corner post of its stall. He pulled the horse's head toward him, checked its teeth, and then released the animal, which immediately began to chew the stall post again.

Cimarron checked the horse's legs, looked at its shod hooves, and then left the stall.

"You want him?" the liveryman asked.

"I don't like his bad habit of cribbing," Cimarron

answered. "He'll wind up bruising, maybe cutting his mouth if he keeps on like that. Then he won't take a bit on account of his mouth and lips'll be too sore to tolerate it."

"You could try driving wedges in between some of his teeth to break him of his cribbing habit," suggested the liveryman.

"That's liable to cause more problems than it cures," Cimarron pointed out.

"Tell you what," said the liveryman after a moment's hesitation. "I was going to ask fifteen dollars for that bay, but since he cribs, I'll knock a dollar off the price. How's that suit you?"

"Were you to knock five dollars off the price, it'd suit me fine," Cimmaron countered.

"But I paid ten dollars for the nag," exclaimed the liveryman.

"Let's go, Murdoch." Cimarron headed for the door.

"Wait!" cried the liveryman. "I'll pare my profit to the bare bones. I'll turn him over to you for twelve dollars."

"Throw in a packsaddle, mister," Cimarron said, "and you've sold yourself a horse."

Later, as Cimarron, with Murdoch at his side, led the rope-haltered and headstalled bay out of the livery, Murdoch muttered, "Maybe we should have passed that bay by and tried to find a better pack animal somewhere else."

"There isn't any somewhere else here in Fort Smith," Cimarron pointed out. "That livery's the only place to buy and sell horseflesh for miles around. Besides, I can cure this animal of his cribbing habit."

"How?"

"Easy. I'll get me a length of leather and put some tacks in it and use it as a throat latch on this old fellow. That'll curb his cribbing, you can count on it."

They made their way to the merchantile, where they left the bay and their horses tied to the hitchrail outside. They spent less than fifteen minutes in the store; when they emerged carrying boxes and gunnysacks filled with supplies, they found the bay busily engaged in cribbing one of the uprights supporting the hitchrail.

Cimarron promptly fashioned the tack-embedded throat latch he had mentioned to Murdoch, and fastened it around the bay's neck. The horse pulled back its lips to reveal its teeth and bent its head to begin cribbing again. But it suddenly raised its head, drew away from the wooden upright, and nickered. It tried again to crib and again it withdrew from the upright, shaking its head and snorting.

"It works, what you did," Murdoch commented.

"Sure it does."

"How does it?"

"On account of when a horse starts to crib he stiffens up the muscles in his throat and neck. That throat latch I made—the tacks I stuck into it—they bite into his neck when he stiffens up his muscles so he learns real quick to stop cribbing so he won't feel any pain."

Cimarron swung into the saddle and Murdoch boarded his buckskin. Minutes later, both men, with Cimarron leading the bay, were heading for the ferry that would carry them across the Arkansas River to the eastern border of Indian Territory.

An hour after the sun had set that evening, they made camp near the junction of the Arkansas and Canadian rivers. While Murdoch stripped and hobbled their horses, Cimarron built a fire and filled the kettle and coffee pot Murdoch had bought at the mercantile with water drawn from the Canadian. Twenty minutes later, he ladled out portions of boiled rice mixed with raisins onto his and Murdoch's tin plates.

"This spotted pup," Murdoch commented, using the trail hands' name for the rice-and-raisin mixture, "is tastier than I ever remember it being."

"That's due to the pinch of ginger I stirred into it once all the water had boiled away."

"I'll have seconds if there's more left in the pot," Murdoch said some time later when he had emptied his plate.

"Help yourself." Cimarron continued eating and staring at the purpled peaks of the San Bois Mountains off to the south.

"Tell me something, Cimarron," Murdoch began when he had refilled his plate. "How long have you been a deputy marshal out here in the Territory?"

"Nigh on to five years."

"Five years. That's quite a while. Most deputies, judging from what I've heard, don't last nearly that long in the job. They either get gun-shy or find a more lucrative means of earning a living."

"Or else they team up with a woman somewhere and take to raising kids and crops."

"But you never did."

"Nope, I never did."

"Nor have I."

"You like what you do too much to settle down, I take it?"

"I like it well enough." Cimarron noted the eagerness in Murdoch's tone as the bounty hunter added, "I get rather a kick out of running men down."

"Know what you mean. I get a good feeling when I'm out after some owlhoot or other. It's a quickening in the blood like I used to get every spring after my ma had filled me full of sulfur and molasses. It's a lot like the feeling a man gets when he's out hunting. It's a prickly feeling all up and down the back of your neck. A sort of shivery feeling that sets your heart to pounding up against your ribs like it's getting ready to bust out on you."

"And when you've finally run your man down and you have him in your sights—that's a feeling that can get a strong hold on a man," Murdoch mused.

Cimarron opened a can of peaches, which he shared with Murdoch. "It's not just the hunting I like," he ventured. "It's the living free and being able to wander about as easy as the wind does. I like that. I don't take to towns. I get the feeling when I'm in them sometimes that they're closing in on me, boxing me in. But out here a man's got room to move about in and breathe easy."

"How many men have you run down?" Murdoch suddenly asked.

Cimarron gave him a sidelong glance before answering, "I don't keep count. Do you?"

Murdoch smiled. "I've trailed eleven men. So far. I've trailed them through the Big Thicket down in Texas and up across the plains of Kansas. And I caught every last one of them in the end. Al Tolliver was my last catch. I finally ran him down right here in Indian Territory."

"He holed up here to stay clear of the Arkansas authorities, did he?"

"He did."

"Lots of men do the same thing. The Territory's a hidey-hole for more snakes from places like Texas and Arkansas and even further away than any snake-chasers like us can count. Where'd you run him down at?"

"Just south of Sasakwa in Seminole Nation."

"You said, as I recall, that Tolliver was working with a partner."

"He was. With a man named Dusty Atkins."

"But Atkins, you said, gave you the slip."

Murdoch nodded and ate the last of the peaches on his plate. "Atkins was with Tolliver the day I caught up with them. But there was a gunfight, as you might expect, and during it Atkins made his getaway. Tolliver," Murdoch commented wryly, "wasn't so fortunate. I took him back to Arkansas and collected my five hundred dollars for him and he was hanged.

"I've been keeping my eyes and ears open since then for news of the whereabouts of Dusty Atkins. Of course, the bounty on his head is a lot less than was offered for the apprehension of Tolliver. It's only two hundred dollars. But I hope to collect it one day nonetheless."

"Two hundred dollars is nothing to sneeze at. I wish they'd've paid that kind of money to me for deputying like I'd been doing for so long. But they didn't. They paid hardly enough for a man—and a thrifty man at that—to keep his body and soul together. Which is why I quit the damned job."

"You're not a deputy anymore?"

"Nope. I turned in my badge not long before I ran into you and Tolliver."

"What were you planning on doing? I mean, how did you intend to earn a living?"

"I hadn't the least notion, to tell you the truth." Cimarron poured coffee into two cups and handed one to Murdoch. "So it was a good thing you offered me this job of siding you on the way to Wetumka."

Murdoch sipped his coffee. Then, "It didn't occur to me before, for the simple reason that I assumed you were merely taking time out from your regular job to accompany me to Wetumka as I asked you to do. But now that you say you're at loose ends as far as gainful employment is concerned . . ." Murdoch thoughtfully stroked his chin in silence for a moment before continuing. "What would you say to making our partnership permanent, Cimarron?"

"You mean throw in with you and hunt men for the bounty on their heads?"

"You said a little while ago that you enjoyed hunting owlhoots when you were a deputy. Hunting them for bounty is much the same thing as what you were doing before, as we discussed in the drugstore back in Fort Smith. And my business, judging by what you've just told me, is far more remunerative than yours ever was."

"I appreciate your offer, Murdoch, but I'm just not ready to make a move in any permanent direction, not at the moment I'm not."

"I can understand that. A man needs time to kick over the traces once and for all before he can see his way clear to doing something else. But I'd like to point out to you if I may, Cimarron, that you could do worse. Then, too, there is another factor you should consider."

"What factor's that?"

"The matter of a man's skills. Sometimes when a fellow finds himself out of work, he has to take just about any job that comes to hand to put food on his table. And the job he takes may not suit the skills he's honed over the years, not to mention that it might not suit him temperamentally, which is, I venture to say, almost as important. The point is, Cimarron, were you to start partnering with me, you would be using the very same skills that you have been using during your days as a deputy. Your skill with a gun, your cunning in trailing a man to whatever lair he's chosen for himself, your physical strength and endurance that come into play during the long days and nights in the wildnerness—"

"What you say's true enough, but like I said, I'm not sure yet what trail I'll take once we get to Wetumka."

"I hope you'll give my proposition some thought, Cimarron. I hope you won't reject it out of hand. I know that I, for one, would welcome such a partnership. The two of us, I'm absolutely certain, would make an unbeatable team. And as for the bounty money we'd collect, well, we could split whatever we jointly earn on a fifty-fifty basis."

"That's fair enough, I reckon."

"Then you'll think the matter over?"

"I will." Cimarron emptied his cup and then got up. He picked up the plates and utensils and carried them down to the river, where he knelt on the bank and proceeded to wash them. He dried them on the grass and then, on his way back to the fire, stopped to check the horses. When he was satisfied that they were not too tightly hobbled and that Murdoch had left them in an area where there was decent browse, he made his way back to the fire, which was burning more brightly now because Murdoch had added more wood to it.

He hunkered down, poured himself another cup of coffee, and drank slowly as Murdoch spread his tarp and bedroll on the ground not far from the fire.

Bounty hunter.

The term bounced about in his brain. I could do it, he thought. I could do it easy. Have done it once, as a matter of fact. He thought back to the time when he had been hired by Harriet Becker to run down her husband. He thought about the cold cash she had offered him for her husband's cold corpse. Bad business that, he remembered. But bounty hunting with Murdoch wouldn't be like that situation had been, he told himself. This would all be on the up and up. Everything up front and aboveboard this time. And Murdoch was right. He knows I have what it takes to do it. The pay'd be good, a helluva lot better than what I've been earning for the past nigh on to five years, he mused. So what for am I hesitating? he asked himself.

Cimarron couldn't come up with any better answer than that something about Murdoch, or maybe about the idea of bounty hunting—something he couldn't put a finger on or a name to—made him decidedly skittish about the proposal.

Bounty hunting, he thought as he stared into the flickering flames of the campfire and sipped his coffee, it's no far cry from being a lawman like I've been up till now. So it wouldn't be that much of a switch for me, like Murdoch said.

Lawman.

The figure rose up from the flames—the lawman Cimarron dreaded facing again and who would not be banished. Cimarron tried to blink the man away, but he remained standing steadily in the fire. When Cimarron tried to turn his head, tried to look away, the man slowly raised a hand, pointed an accusing finger, and spoke the name that Cimarron had abandoned that long ago day when he had fired his gun and a man had died.

No. The word, the denial, was a whisper in Cimarron's mind, but it didn't work. The lawman continued to glow red in the flames, his eyes blazing, his lips writhing as he muttered accusations, his indicting finger pointing at Cimarron . . .

. . . who remembered once again that awful day. Remembered the bank in the Texas Panhandle. Himself down on one knee in front of the iron safe as he scooped both hard and folding money into a sack. One of his confederates was shouting—something about the law. He turned swiftly, the gun in his hand rising, and saw the man silhouetted in the doorway with the sun behind him, the featureless man who was now flickering in the flames of the campfire.

He fired.

The man in the doorway crumbled, his knees buckled, his head dropped like a flower in a drought. He fell, hit the wooden floor, and lay there without moving.

He was up then and running for the door, the sack full of stolen money in one hand, his still-smoking gun in the other. He ran past the frightened tellers and bank patrons.

But he halted before he reached the door. He turned and looked down, because the glimpse of the man he had just killed had momentarily frozen him in his tracks. He cringed. His flesh grew cold. It crawled. It oozed sweat as he stared speechlessly at his father, who wore a sheriff's star. He somehow managed to speak, succeeded in asking the questions that were tearing his mind to shreds.

The terrified bank patrons and tellers answered him, their words fragmented by their fear of him.

The sheriff had come to their town years ago after his wife had died. They had found him to be both a good neighbor and a good man. They had asked him to be their sheriff. He had taken the job.

Cimarron's mind whirled. His ma—dead. His pa—dead. He had killed his pa without knowing who he was shooting at, because his target's face had been hidden in the bank's backlighted doorway. He tried to tell himself it had been an accident. He hadn't meant to kill his father. But he had meant to kill the lawman in the doorway who would have—would he have?—killed him if he hadn't acted first.

He turned and fled from the bank. Outside, he tossed the sack full of money to one of the other outlaws and rode away alone.

Soon he discovered he was not alone.

A man was riding his backtrail. A dead man. And that dead lawman called out to him, called him by the name he knew he would never dare use again if he wanted to remain a free man, and asked him, Why?

And the question, that one awful word, unlocked a box from which memories spilled like long-forgotten toys that had belonged to the boy he had once been.

He remembered his ma, and how she would tousle his hair and tell him he was the apple of her eye. He recalled how she could plow a furrow straighter than any man, and how she could bake an apple pie that was sweeter, so said his pa, than the voices of an entire army of angels.

She'd try to console him when he had one of his all-too-frequent clashes with his pa.

"He means you well, boy," she would say. "He wants the whole world for you, boy. But he knows you won't get it do you not grow straight and true. Why must you set out to be such a trial to him?"

"All I did was I said a bad word and he up and whupped me for it, and the fact is he says the same word all the time. It isn't fair, Ma."

"Neither's this old world we all find ourselves plunked down in," his ma retorted without anger. "Your pa's out to see to it that you grow up to be better than him. But, like him, a true believer in the word of the Lord and a walker on the straight and narrow path to salvation."

"Pa ought to fret more about his own failings than he does about mine."

"You be willful, boy. So willful you won't let yourself understand your pa a'tall. His chance, it's long since past. He's grown. And growing old. You, you're like a young sapling that can be bent to grow any which way a body wants it to. Your pa, he wants you to grow up righteous."

"Well, I ain't about to put up with that leather belt of his on my bare behind no more, Ma. I *won't* put up with it."

He wondered if his ma had grieved when she found him gone that rainy morning not long after their brief and fruitless discussion. He supposed she had, because

53

he knew she loved him. He also knew that a woman like his ma, with a heart as big as a barn, could do naught else but grieve over a loved one lost to death or the real world beyond the homeplace in central Texas.

The places he went to in the years following his flight flickered through his mind now just as the flames of the campfire flickered with the image of his dead father.

Denver, where he had killed a man who had challenged his three-card monte game and where he had done hard time in the federal penitentiary. The Barbary Coast, where he consorted with its painted women and drunken sailors. He remembered all the places and all the times, and he knew himself for a stranger in each one of them. Finally, the bank in the Texas Panhandle on that fateful day. And the dead father forever on his backtrail, who asked a question that could never be answered because how can a man speak of the love he had for a man he has murdered?

Dead lips called his name from the fire. He looked into the eyeless face and flinched. He closed his eyes and asked—someone, anyone—for mercy. It was granted him, for when he opened his eyes again, the flames were all he saw.

Lawman, he thought. Like father, like son, he thought.

He put down his empty cup, got up quickly, and went to where Murdoch had earlier piled the gear he had stripped from the three horses before hobbling them for the night. He picked up his saddle and placed it on the ground against the thick trunk of a cottonwood. After spreading his tarp and blanket, he removed his cartridge belt and lay down, placing his .44 next to his head. He drew his hat down over his face and wrapped his blanket around him to keep out the November night that had grown so cold. He fell asleep almost at once and dreamed a disturbing dream of a strange country where the night sky was filled with tin stars, all of which had the word *sheriff* engraved on their glittering surfaces.

* * *

Cimarron awoke just after dawn the next morning and shivered. His face and hair were wet as a result of the dew that had formed during the night. When he sat up, tilted his hat back on his head, and looked around, he found the land shrouded in a dense fog that was rising from the river. Through it, he could just barely make out the huddled shape of the still-sleeping Murdoch.

He stretched, yawned, and got to his feet. After folding his tarp and blanket, he made his way to the riverbank, where he knelt and drank. He splashed cold water on his face and shivered again as the fog seeped beneath his clothes and turned his flesh clammy.

A sound from behind him caused him to rise and turn, his right hand going for his gun. But it was only Murdoch getting to his feet and making rumbling noises deep in his throat, like some misshapen beast who had become lost in the fog and was angrily seeking a way out of it.

Cimarron returned to the dead fire and rekindled it with fresh fuel. As its flames flared up, red against the gray sheets of shifting fog, he held his hands out to it to warm them.

Murdoch joined him and did the same. "What a morning," the man muttered. "It's as cold as a welldigger's ass."

"You call this cold, do you?"

"You don't?"

"Nope. It's nothing to compare with the cold I remember from the time I was living in a lone shack up on a ranch in Colorado. It was toward the tail end of January, as I recollect. It was so cold that time that the flame of the candle I was using froze stiff and I had to wait till it thawed before I could put it out. Then, once the sun came up, it got real hot and the corn I'd put out for the stock started to pop. My horse thought that popcorn was snow and almost froze to death on me."

Murdoch managed a thin smile.

"I'll cook us some breakfast," Cimarron volunteered.

Both men sat on the ground by the fire and drank

coffee, Murdoch with his blanket wrapped around his shoulders. Salt pork sizzled noisily in a frying pan and carrots boiled in a kettle. Cimarron put down his cup and added chunks of peeled potatoes to the boiling water.

When the food was ready, both men ate in silence. Cimarron watched the fog drift as the dimly seen sun rose and began to burn it off. The fog was almost completely gone by the time they finished eating. While Murdoch washed the breakfast things, Cimarron saw to the horses. First, he unhobbled them and drove them down to the river to drink. When Murdoch rejoined him and handed over the breakfast things, Cimarron proceeded to fasten the sawbuck packsaddle on the horse Murdoch had bought. He carefully fastened the rig's double cinches so that they wouldn't cause sores on the horse's barrel. Then, working deftly with the rig's wooden crossbucks, short thin bars, and his manila rope, he soon had the load in place.

He was saddling his black and Murdoch was kicking out the fire when he thought he saw movement among a stand of shin oaks growing between the river and the camp. He narrowed his eyes and kept them fastened on the spot where he thought he had seen something move. Had it been a shifting, a turning of leaves as the wind lifted them? A deer moving among the trees? An alteration of the light, tricking him into thinking he had seen—something else?

His hand eased toward his saddle scabbard and came to rest on the stock of his '73 Winchester.

In the distance, Murdoch let out a lusty oath.

Cimarron's hand closed on his rifle's stock. He turned to find a man sitting astride a dun and holding a carbine on Murdoch a score of yards from the ashes of the campfire. Cimarron was about to pull his Winchester free of its scabbard, but before he could do so, the mounted man swung the barrel of his carbine toward him and barked, "Hands off that gun, Deputy."

Deputy? How come he knows me, Cimarron wondered, when I've never seen hide nor hair of him?

"Drop that gunbelt."

Cimarron hesitated.

"Move away from that horse," ordered the man with the carbine.

Cimarron, as Murdoch glanced nervously at him, stepped away from the black. He stared hard at Murdoch, almost glaring at him as he tried to convey his thoughts to the bounty hunter. The mounted gunman ordered Murdoch to drop his gun. Murdoch did so, giving Cimarron a second glance that betrayed both anger and a flickering of fear.

The man with the carbine, his face impassive, turned toward Cimarron. Without raising his weapon, he fired a single shot, which bit into the ground directly in front of Cimarron's boots, spraying them with dirt.

Cimarron, as the gunman's finger tightened again on his carbine's trigger, unholstered his gun and let it drop to the ground. "Who might you be, mister?" he asked in a voice that was edged with anger.

"Dusty Atkins." The answer to Cimarron's question had come not from the armed man but from Murdoch.

For a split second the name meant nothing to Cimarron. Then he remembered Murdoch telling him that Tolliver had had a partner in the robbery of the bank during which Tolliver had shot a teller to death. The partner's name had been, he now recalled, Dusty Atkins.

"What business have you here?" Cimarron asked Atkins, although he was sure he knew the answer to his question. He wanted to stall to give himself time to think of how he could get himself and Murdoch out from under Atkin's gun.

"It's not business that brings me here," Atkins answered, his thin lips cracking in what might have been a smile. "It's pleasure. The pure pleasure of killing that filthy bounty hunter there who booted my partner through death's door—and a conniving deputy marshal right along with him."

Atkins shifted in his saddle. The sunlight sent shadows scurrying across the bony face in which sooty eyes glittered. He was a gaunt man who looked ill-fed. He also looked ill-groomed. His straight hair, the color of mud, was greasy, reaching almost to his shoulders. His ears were large and angled out from the sides of his head. He wore a sweat-stained gray stetson, a black shirt, twill trousers, and a canvas jacket.

"How come you know me and my work?" Cimarron asked Atkins. He took a short step backward so that his cartridge belt lay on the ground directly in front of him.

"The bartender back in Fort Smith told me you had hooked up with Murdoch here. He said you boys were heading down to Wetumka in Creek Nation. He said he heard just about every word you two said to each other, and he was glad to repeat some of those words for me when I offered him a brace of double eagles to do that very thing. And then the liveryman, he said he'd sold you two a pack horse, and he also mentioned where you were on your way to." Atkins threw back his head and guffawed.

Cimarron swiftly dropped to his knees and slid his .44 out of its oiled holster. He was in the act of cocking the gun when Murdoch screamed, "Don't Cimarron!"

He looked to his left. Bill Tolliver sat aboard a paint that was pawing the ground directly behind Murdoch. He saw the six-gun in Tolliver's hand aimed directly at Murdoch's skull; then he remembered thinking he'd seen movement in among the shin oaks back by the river. He saw the joyless twisted smile on Tolliver's face and he knew it was Tolliver who had been hiding in the trees. He dropped his Colt and stood up.

Tolliver gestured with the barrel of his gun, and Cimarron stepped back from his dropped weapon.

"Taking you two was easy," Tolliver said, his smile vanishing. "I thought I'd have me some trouble doing the job, which is why I rounded up Dusty to side me. But it looks like I could have done the job all by my lonesome."

"You no doubt could have, Tolliver," Dusty agreed, "but I'm real glad you invited me to come along with you, because I want to put some lead in that bounty-hunter too. I want to pay him back for what he did to Al."

Tolliver gave Murdoch, who found himself between Tolliver's six-gun and Atkins' carbine, a murderous glare. "Between the two of us, Dusty, we can put so much lead into that bounty-hunter that he'll sink right down into the ground from the weight of it. Which is not such a bad idea, since it'll save us the task of burying him."

"I'd not bury the bastard," Atkins said. "I'd as soon leave him for the coyotes and buzzards. Leave him to his own kind, if you follow me."

"Atkins," Cimarron began, "you and Tolliver both know that what Murdoch did was legal. He brought in a wanted man. What you two sound like you're fixing to do is illegal. It's cold-blooded murder. You'll have the law out after you, and sooner or later you'll both end up stretching rope."

"That prospect sets me to shaking in my boots," Atkins declared mockingly. "In fact, it scares me so much I might miss my target on account of the way my hands are trembling."

But when Atkins raised his carbine to his shoulder, took aim at Murdoch, and fired, he didn't miss.

4

Murdoch gave a loud grunt as Atkins' round slammed through the flesh of his upper left arm. He was spun around by the force of the bullet and almost lost his balance.

"My turn," cried Tolliver with glee in his voice and a smile on his face.

As Tolliver cocked his six-gun, Murdoch gave an alarmed cry and started to run.

As Tolliver's revolver and Atkins' carbine swung like weather vanes away from him and toward the fleeing Murdoch, Cimarron threw himself to the ground and retrieved his .44. Lying prone, both hands gripping the butt of his gun, he fired at Tolliver.

His shot missed, because the man put heels to his horse and moved swiftly out after Murdoch. Before Cimarron could fire again, Tolliver let out an angry yell and, turning in the saddle, fired at him. But Cimarron had rolled over, and the shot buried itself in the ground where he had been only a moment ago. He sprang to his feet and raced toward his horse, which was nervously backing away, its ears flicking up and down. He heard a shot *ping* past him and knew by its sound that it had come from Atkins' carbine. He half-turned and fired a snapshot at Atkins, who had turned his horse and was starting to come after him. Atkins cursed and drew rein. Cimarron fired at him again, his round causing Atkins' horse suddenly to swerve sharply to the right and almost go down.

When he reached his black, Cimarron vaulted into the saddle, turned the horse, and went galloping directly toward Atkins, who was struggling to maintain control of his mount. Tolliver had given up his pursuit of Murdoch, who was now nowhere in sight, and had started back toward Atkins.

Cimarron fired three shots in rapid succession without taking careful aim, hoping at least to drive off both men if he failed to down them. His hope was realized as both Tolliver and Atkins suddenly veered off to avoid colliding with Cimarron, who was rapidly bearing down on them, his empty Colt now holstered and his Winchester in his hand. He made straight for the waist-high pile of granite boulders in the distance, believing that Murdoch must have taken shelter behind them since there was no other cover visible in the immediate vicinity. Reaching them, he was relieved to find that Murdoch had indeed gone to ground behind the natural breastwork. He leapt from his saddle and crouched down beside Murdoch as his black cantered on, then stopped and dropped its head to graze.

"Here they come," Murdoch muttered. "And I don't have a goddamned gun!"

Cimarron handed him his Winchester, then quickly thumbed cartridges from his belt and filled the six empty chambers of his .44.

Both men fired at the same time. Cimarron's shot grazed the neck of Tolliver's paint.

The paint screamed, reared, and then went racing away into the woods. Tolliver, thrown from the saddle, lost his gun as he hit the ground.

Murdoch, whose first shot had been a wild one that had hit no target, fired a second time. This time he hit Tolliver, who had gotten to his feet and was picking up his gun, in the right leg. Tolliver's knees buckled as Murdoch's next round plowed into the ground directly behind him. But he managed to hobble toward the only cover available to him—the stand of shin oaks in which he had hidden earlier.

Cimarron fired at Atkins, who was galloping away, but Atkins was already out of range. "Give me that rifle." Cimarron tore his weapon from Murdoch's hands.

Murdoch swore at him and tried to get it back. "Tolliver's getting away," he yelled as he continued to struggle for possession of the gun. Murdoch let out a yell of pain when Cimarron angrily slammed his hand against the granite rocks, forcing him to let go of the gun.

Cimarron rammed the stock of his Winchester against his shoulder and was about to take aim when he realized that during his struggle with Murdoch, Atkins had apparently ridden up to the wounded Tolliver and helped the man up behind the cantle of his saddle. Before Cimarron could fire, Atkins' dun bore both men into the protective cover of the shin oaks, where they disappeared from sight.

"God damn it!" Murdoch yelled. "Why the hell didn't you let me do for Tolliver when I had the chance?"

"Shut up, Murdoch, and listen to me. We've got to flush that pair out of those woods over there."

"Where the hell are you going?"

Cimarron, who had risen and was retreating from the rocks, answered over his shoulder, "To get those two. I'm going to circle around and come in on them from behind. What you do in the meantime is you keep firing on them from time to time."

Murdoch hunkered down behind the rock and fired a shot, while Cimarron mounted and rode east, circling around in a wide arc until he could barely make out the edge of the western boundary of the woods. He rode halfway up to them, then drew rein and dismounted. Leaving the black ground-hitched, he made his way on foot into the trees, where little sunlight penetrated and the air was cold and damp.

He took cover behind the trunk of a tree and listened carefully, but could hear no one moving in the woods; only the occasional sound of distant and sporadic gunfire came from the rifle he had left with Murdoch. He heard no answering fire from Tolliver and Atkins. Had Murdoch managed to hit both men? Was that why he heard no return fire? He eased out from behind the tree and moved cautiously forward, his eyes roving to the right and left as he searched for his quarry. But he found no sign of either man—not until he reached a spot where the trees were thinner and he was able to make out the hoof prints of two horses on a broad patch of clear ground that wasn't littered with humus. He scanned the soft ground and saw the imprint of boots.

He walked a few feet in one direction and then a few feet in the opposite direction, his eyes on the ground, until he found sign that told him which way the two men had gone. They had headed south, he realized. While he was wasting time doubling back to try to take them, they had not remained in the woods as he had believed they would but instead apparently caught Tolliver's horse and ridden away, making good their escape before he had even entered the woods.

He went back to where he had left his horse, swung into the saddle, and then reentered the woods. He was about to leave the cover of the trees when a rifle round whistled past his right ear. He cursed and shouted Murdoch's name at the top of his voice.

Cimarron's rifle in his hands, Murdoch slowly rose from behind the rocky breastwork in the distance.

"Don't shoot," Cimarron shouted, then moved his horse out of the woods and went galloping toward the pile of rocks.

When he reached them, he dismounted. "They're gone," he told the bounty hunter. "I took it for granted that they'd hole up in those woods back there, but it turns out I was wrong."

"Let's go get them."

Cimarron shook his head. "They're heading south and that's out of our way. What we'd best do is put some distance in between us and them."

"You figure they'll come after us again." Murdoch had made a statement, not asked a question.

"They might, once they catch their breath. But by now they know what they're up against. They know we'll not be taken easy, and they also know, or ought to know, that we'll be real wary from here on in."

"I don't know, Cimarron," Murdoch said moodily. "Maybe we'd better trail those two and get rid of them once and for all."

"I didn't come on this trip to kill anybody, Murdoch. So, if they leave us be, I won't have to. If they don't . . ." He left his sentence unfinished. Then, "By the way, we, you and me, made a couple of mistakes back in Fort Smith."

"Mistakes?"

"We shouldn't have talked so free in front of that bar dog back there so he could find out where we were headed and tell anybody who happened to ask him about us, as it turns out Tolliver and Atkins did. Same thing holds true for the liveryman. You oughtn't to have told him where we were headed when he asked. By the way, how's your arm?"

"Not too bad. The bleeding's stopped."

"The bullet—is it in you?"

"It went through."

"You'd best mosey on down to the river and wash your wound so it don't get infected. Then you can bind it up to keep it clean. Once you've done your doctoring, we'll ride north."

"North? Why north? Wetumka's southwest of us."

"I know that. But what we'd best do at this juncture is lay down a false trail for Tolliver and Atkins to follow if and when they should decide to come after us again."

Cimarron took his rifle from Murdoch and reloaded both guns with cartridges he thumbed from his belt.

Murdoch commented, "I see you're a thrifty man, Cimarron."

Cimarron looked up at him and nodded. "With this

rifle and revolver of mine I only have to buy and tote forty-four–forty cartridges. Saves some money; besides which I'm partial to the '73 and this here Frontier Colt of mine. Both guns stand a man in good stead when the going gets tough."

Murdoch left him to retrieve the gun he had been forced to drop and made his way down to the river. Cimarron bridled and saddled his black and then got Murdoch's buckskin ready to ride.

When Murdoch returned, both men swung into the saddle and rode toward the river, Cimarron leading the pack horse. They forded the Canadian and rode north into Cherokee Nation for nearly an hour. North of the town of Mackey, Cimarron turned his horse and, followed by Murdoch, rode due west until they came to the Illinois River.

Cimarron rode into the river and reversed his course, heading south through the shallows. When he spotted a rocky expanse of ground on the river's western bank that would not show sign of their leaving the river at that point, he rode out onto dry ground. Then he and Murdoch again headed toward Wetumka, their ultimate destination.

As they crossed from Cherokee Nation into Creek Nation, Cimarron held up a hand and they halted.

"What is it?" Murdoch asked in an uneasy voice. "You see somebody?"

Cimarron pointed.

"Well, I'll be damned," Murdoch exclaimed. "Look at those two have at it!"

Cimarron watched as the eagle and coyote he had spotted in the distance waged their fierce battle over the lifeless and bloody body of a dead jackrabbit, which one of them had apparently killed and both apparently wanted.

The eagle seemed to be winning the battle. It swooped down on the coyote, who met its outstretched claws with an angry snapping of its jaws, but to no avail. The eagle's talons closed on the coyote's spine and the still-snapping coyote was lifted into the air only to be dropped from a height of nearly fifteen feet. The coyote hit the ground hard, rolled over, and then was up and racing back to the dead jack. It reached the prize at the same time that the eagle swooped down once again to seize its rival. Again the coyote, caught in the grip of the eagle's talons, was lifted into the air and again the eagle dropped its enemy to the ground. This time a large furry piece of the coyote's hide remained clinging to the eagle's talons.

The coyote, in no way discouraged, recovered from its fall, shook itself, let out a ragged howl, and went racing back to the jack, which it seized in its teeth. It began to run with the jack in its jaws, but the eagle plummeted down out of the sky and stabbed the fleeing coyote with its beak before rising into the air again on its great wings.

Twice more the eagle repeated its maneuver. The coyote, wounded and bleeding badly, did not relinquish the jack. When the eagle came after it a third time, it let the jack fall and crouched down. As the eagle came closer, the coyote sprang up and its jaws snapped shut on the bird's throat. The eagle struggled to free itself, its wings thrashing wildly. But the coyote held firmly to its prey, letting itself be lifted a foot or two off the ground from time to time as the eagle fought hard to escape its would-be killer.

Minutes passed as the struggle continued. At last the eagle's wings began to beat feebly, and the blood that flowed from its throat gradually slowed and then finally stopped when the bird's heart did. As the eagle flopped lifeless on the ground, the coyote maintained its grip on its prey. More minutes passed. At last, apparently satisfied that its enemy was dead, the coyote released the eagle, picked up the dead jack in its teeth, and loped out of sight behind a low rise.

"Tolliver," Cimarron said. "Atkins."

"What are you talking about?" Murdoch asked him with a frown on his face.

"Tolliver could be the eagle," Cimarron answered. "Atkins the coyote. You and me the jack. Tolliver and Atkins are no doubt as determined to get us as that bird and beast were to make a meal out of that jack."

Cimarron moved out and Murdoch followed him. They had gone less than a mile and were just topping a rise when Cimarron muttered an oath as he spotted a spring wagon in the distance. It was careening out of control, and its driver, a woman, was holding tightly to the seat with both hands, the reins dragging along the ground beneath the wagon as the two horses pulling it dashed madly on.

Cimarron put heels to his horse and went galloping down the rise, heading for the wagon. The wind whipped his hat brim and his hair as he rode, his eyes on the wagon up ahead of him and the shrilly screaming woman. Within minutes, he had come abreast of the wagon on the left. When she saw him, the woman stopped screaming and shouted, "*Help!*" He swung his left leg over his saddle horn, kicked his right foot free of its stirrup, and leapt. He caught the left side of the wagon's seat with both hands and hauled himself up until he was sitting next to the woman. He looked down at the dangling reins and then reached for the brake only to discover that its shoe had been broken off, rendering it useless.

"I've got to get the reins," he yelled to the woman over the loud pounding of the team's hooves and the rattling of the wagon's whirling wheels.

Her face blanched as he began to climb over the front of the seat and the horses raced crazily on, their manes streaming out behind them, their legs pounding the ground, their ears laid back, and their teeth clamped tightly on the bits in their mouths. He was just about to lower himself onto the wagon's swaying wooden tongue when the woman screamed again. He glanced over his shoulder at her. She pointed straight ahead of her and Cimarron glanced in that direction, the wagon swaying precariously as it rolled over uneven ground. He saw the fallen red maple that the horses were careening toward as if they were unaware of the obstacle looming in their path.

He dropped down onto the wagon tongue and bent over, reaching for the reins. As he did so, the team suddenly swerved, and he was thrown up against the sweaty hip of the horse on his right. He managed to right himself just as both horses veered sharply to the left and went dashing, their heads bobbing and their nostrils flaring, around the deadfall.

Cimarron got ready to make another try for the trailing reins as dirt kicked up by the horses's hooves flew up into his face and almost blinded him. He wiped his eyes with the back of one hand and, blinking to clear his vision, looked down at the reins bouncing along the ground far below him. He was suddenly thrown forward, almost falling to the ground as the horses rounded a bend and galloped onward.

He steadied himself, then froze as he saw the rim of a canyon directly ahead. Behind him, the woman screamed. He knew the horses would not be able to stop in time. There was too little ground left between them and the canyon's rim; their speed was such that they would not have time to turn even if they became aware of the danger lying directly in their path. He could think of only one thing to do to try to stop their headlong flight.

He drew his gun, took aim as the wagon bounced beneath him, and fired once. The horse on the right went down, a bullet in its brain. Cimarron was about to fire at the horse on the left when it slowed abruptly because it was now having to drag the dead body of the other horse as well as the wagon.

He held on as tightly as he could with one hand as the wagon rocked from side to side, then finally came to a shuddering standstill. He relaxed his grip and holstered his gun, his eyes on the canyon's rim less than twenty yards away. He climbed back upon the seat, where the woman was slumped, her face buried in her hands and her shoulders shaking as she sobbed.

"It's all over," he told her. "You don't have to be fearful anymore. Here, I'll help you down." He jumped down to the ground and then held his hands up to help the woman climb down from the wagon.

"Oh, I'm ever so grateful to you," she exclaimed as she reached the ground and looked up at him. "If you hadn't come along when you did . . ." she buried her face in her hands again.

"Glad to be of help. Are you all right?"

The woman took her hands away from her face. "Yes, I think so. I'm just terribly upset. I hope you'll forgive me for acting so foolishly."

She was, despite her strained expression, an attractive woman. Her eyes were large and dark blue, and they seemed to glow with an inner light as she faced Cimarron. Her lips were full, and the tip of her nose had a slight lift to it that gave her a pert look. Her complexion was smooth and creamy and clearly had not been exposed to much sunlight or inclement weather.

Her body was lithe despite her large breasts and the feminine flare of her hips.

She was wearing a two-piece gray velvet traveling suit. The hem of her full skirt and the cuffs and bottom of her jacket sported fancy embroidery done in black and white. Round ebony buttons ran in a prim row from her chin down to her waist. Topping her upswept and pinned auburn hair was a flat-topped straw hat, which was bordered with a band as blue as her eyes and rather jauntily trimmed with paper forget-me-nots.

"What happened?" Cimarron asked her.

"I don't really know. Perhaps there was a snake in the grass and it spooked my team, although I didn't see one. But all at once they began to run. I tried my best to stop them, but then, as I tried with both hands to keep the brake on, it broke and I lost my grip on the reins."

"You just stay put while I go check on that horse of yours. I'm real sorry I had to shoot the other one, but

I just couldn't think of any other way to stop us from going head over heels down into that canyon yonder."

"I'm glad you did what you did. You saved my life—both our lives."

Cimarron gave her a grin and went to examine the surviving horse. Then, after inspecting the wagon, he started back to the woman, who was talking animatedly to Murdoch, who had ridden up to her.

". . . and your friend acted so quickly and so decisively," Cimarron heard her say as he approached her. "He was really quite remarkable." He basked then in the warm smile she gave him. He took her hand when she held it out to him and said, "I'm Julia Sinclair."

"Folks call me Cimarron."

"I'm Sam Murdoch, Miss—is it Miss or Mrs. Sinclair?" Murdoch inquired politely.

"It's miss," she answered, delighting Cimarron with her answer.

"Your brake's busted," he told her, "and so's a spoke in your right front wheel."

"Oh, dear, whatever shall I do now?" she lamented. "I've a damaged wagon, a dead horse, and still such a long way to go."

"Where are you headed?" Cimarron asked her.

"I was on my way to Wetumka."

"Well, now!" he crowed happily. "So are me and Murdoch. Give me a little time and I'll see if I can't mend that spoke and brake, and if I can, I'll put my black in with your horse and then we'll be all set to travel to Wetumka together."

"It's really awfully good of you to offer to help me this way," Julia said, and sighed, wearily running the back of a hand across her forehead.

"You look a little peaked, Miss Sinclair," Cimarron observed. "Maybe you could use some rest before we set out again."

"I could indeed."

"There's a road ranch not far from here that's run by an old friend of mine name of Seth Scovill. It's not much of a place but you could get some rest there. So could Murdoch and me."

Murdoch's eyebrows rose. "We haven't time to waste on any road ranch, and you know we don't, Cimarron."

"Murdoch, I'm tuckered," Cimarron lied. "If you want to ride on without me, you're welcome to do that, but I'm going to take Miss Sinclair to Scovill's road ranch, which is straight ahead of us. You're welcome to come to Scovill's with us if you've a mind to."

Murdoch angrily muttered something unintelligible.

Cimarron ignored him and made his way back to the wagon, where he managed to work the dead horse out of the traces. He backed the other horse up and the wagon with it, then replaced the dead horse with his still-saddled and bridled mount.

Once he had the black securely harnessed, he set about repairing the broken spoke in the front wheel, using a piece of a branch he had broken from a tree to serve as a splint, which he lashed in place with a length of rope. Then he carved a thick piece of wood he broke from the same branch, and when he was satisfied that he had fashioned a reasonable facsimile of a brake shoe, he lashed it to the bottom end of the broken brake.

After tying the pack horse to the rear of the wagon, he returned to Julia and Murdoch, who seemed to be ignoring each other, and announced, "We can pull out now. I'll drive the wagon if you don't mind, Miss Sinclair, on account of that brake'll take some favoring till it can be replaced with a brand-new one."

"The wheel you mentioned," Julia said. "The one with the broken spoke. Will it hold?"

"It will. I splinted it and it'll hold for a while." Cimarron helped Julia climb back onto the wagon seat and then he climbed up and sat down beside her. He picked up the reins, which he had earlier wrapped around the brake, and clucked to the team.

"Steady now," he told his black as the animal sidestepped and tossed his head. To Julia he said, "That black of mine's not used to pulling a wagon, and from the way he's acting, I'd say he's not at all happy about having to do it." He kept a tight rein on the team and soon had the black under control, although the animal turned its head several times and gave an amused Cimarron what appeared to him to be a series of highly indignant glances.

Julia laid a tentative hand on Cimarron's right forearm.

"I really shouldn't put you gentlemen out as I'm doing."

"I'm not feeling the least bit put out." He gave Julia a wink.

She gave him a small smile, squeezed his arm, and then withdrew her hand. "I wish there was some way to repay you for your kindness."

There is, Cimarron thought, and felt his shaft begin to stiffen.

"Oh, I know how to do so!"

So do I, Cimarron thought, shifting on the seat to try to hide his rampant erection.

"I shall be gay and tell amusing stories to help us pass the time. I shall be a very merry traveling companion so that neither of you gentlemen will have cause to regret being in my company."

"There's Scovill's place," Cimarron said nearly half an hour later. He pointed to the long log and sod-roofed building, in front of which were two hitch rails. There was an outhouse to its left and a tack shed on its right next to a small corral that contained three horses. Farther away were a springhouse and a chicken coop near which a cow was staked.

"That place looks like it's not fit to slop hogs in," Murdoch remarked sullenly as he rode up beside Cimarron. "I say let's leave the lady here and move on, Cimarron. We can cover another ten, fifteen miles before dark."

"I told you, Murdoch," Cimarron said. "I'm tuckered and this is as far as I go today. I'm looking

forward to spending the night in a
change."

In Julia's if I'm lucky, he thought. Alone if I'm not.

5

Cimarron braked the wagon when they arrived in front of the road ranch, wrapped the reins around the brake handle, and climbed down to the ground. He was helping Julia down when the door of the road ranch opened and an elderly bald man with a bristly brown mustache and long brown beard emerged from it.

"Cimarron," the man exclaimed, hurrying over to the wagon. "You're sure a sight for sore eyes, you are! Where you been keeping yourself, old son? I've not laid an eye on you in many a moon."

"Howdy, Seth," Cimarron greeted the man, and clapped him on the back. "I haven't been out this way lately. How you been keeping, Seth?"

"Tolerable, Cimarron, tolerable. Got the rheumatiz so bad it gives me fits sometimes. But at my age I guess I'm lucky the rheumatiz is all I got. But you don't want to hear about my woes." Seth turned an appraising glance on Julia and Murdoch. "Who be these two, Cimarron? Prisoners or friends of yours?"

"That fellow tethering his mount and pack horse to your hitch rail, Seth, is named Murdoch. Him and me are working together these days."

"He's a deputy too?"

Cimarron shook his head. "Neither am I, as a matter of fact."

"What say you? Not a deputy? What are you talking about, Cimarron?"

"It's a long story, Seth, but I'll cut it short. I got fed up with low pay in a high-risk business, so I quit."

"It's about time you let some sense get into that thick skull of yours. I always told you you were asking for a belly full of lead as a deputy. How many times did I tell you that?"

"More times than I can remember."

"Right. But would you listen? You would not." Seth turned to Murdoch. "He's a bullheaded man. Stubborn as a mule. Once he gets his teeth into something, he won't let go till the last trump, if then." Seth smiled.

So did Cimarron. "The lady, Seth, is Miss Julia Sinclair. The three of us met back along the trail. We're all on our way to Wetumka."

"What business are you and your partner in these days, Cimarron, if you don't mind the curiosity of this old coot?"

"Bounty hunting," Murdoch answered.

Cimarron thought he saw Julia flinch at the sound of the two words.

"Now, that there's a lucrative business if I ever heard of one," Seth declared, stroking his beard and running his other hand over his bald head. "But it can be about as risky as lawdogging," he added with a glance at Cimarron.

"Seth, we could use some hot food and beds for the night," Cimarron stated, wanting to change the subject.

"I can give you both," Seth said eagerly, and then his face fell.

"What's wrong?" Cimarron asked him, noting the man's mournful expression.

"I don't often get ladies as guests, as you well know, Cimarron. I don't have what you could call anything even close to fancy accommodations."

"I'm sure whatever you have will be just fine, Mr. Scovill," Julia interjected.

"All I got in the way of beds," Seth offered doubtfully, "is rough bunks and ticking stuffed full of Montana feathers."

Julia, clearly puzzled, frowned.

"Hay," Cimarron explained to her. "Some plainsmen call hay Montana feathers."

"Come on in, folks, and make yourself to home."

Cimarron and the others followed Seth into the interior of the dirt-floored road ranch, which was dark and dusty. There was a crudely carved long wooden table in the middle of the room with handmade wooden chairs flanking it. Crates, sacks, and barrels of supplies lined one wall and reached the sod ceiling. On either side of the room hung large pieces of canvas draped over ropes. A low fire burned in the stone fireplace, which was flanked on one side by a woodbox and on the other by a tall pile of books. Holes in the log walls where the chinking had fallen out admitted the wind.

"Sit yourself down, folks," Seth directed, "and I'll be about fixing you some vittles."

As Julia and Murdoch seated themselves at the table, Cimarron left the room. Outside, he set to work making a new wagon-wheel spoke. When he had completed that task, he whittled away at a short pole he took from a pile of firewood until he had made a new brake for Julia's wagon. He was completing the task of replacing the broken brake with the new one when Julia appeared in the doorway and called his name. He tested the new brake and then went to where she was waiting for him in the doorway.

"Mr. Scovill says supper is ready," she told him.

"That's news that's good to hear. My belly's as empty as a poor man's purse." He washed up at the pump near the door and then followed Julia inside. He seated himself at the table directly across from her and looked down at the four eggs filling his plate.

"They're almost as fresh as the day they were laid," Scovill advised him. "So there's no need to look askance at them like you're doing."

"I wasn't—"

Scovill interrupted him with "I dip my chickens' eggs in boiling water that's been laced with borox. It coats them and keeps the air out. That way they stay fresh for a long time down in the springhouse. So you can eat them without being afeard of getting poisoned."

Cimarron smiled and began to devour his eggs while Julia across from him and Murdoch beside him did the same.

"Almost forgot," Scovill said as he placed two small tin containers on the table. "Salt's in the blue one, pepper's in the red."

When Cimarron finished his eggs, Scovill whisked the plate out from in front of him and quickly returned it heaped high with slabs of meat.

"Scrapple," Scovill announced as he proceeded to serve slices of the molded and fried pork to Julia and Murdoch.

"This scrapple is really quite good, Mr. Scovill," Julia commented a few minutes later. "It's very tasty."

"I put a little salt in it and a dash of pepper," Scovill said, beaming like a lovestruck boy at Julia. "Sometimes a little garlic too, like in this batch. Pork and garlic go real good together."

"You're quite right, they do," agreed Julia.

"Do you have any coffee, Scovill?" Murdoch asked.

"Pot's on the fire. Be ready in a minute."

"No, thank you," Julia said later as Scovill was about to pour coffee into the cup he had placed beside her empty plate. She dabbed at her lips with a kerchief she took from her sleeve.

"Would you like something else to drink?" he asked her solicitously. "Tea maybe?"

"I don't drink stimulants as a rule," Julia told him, shaking her head.

"How about some nice cold milk? I've got some stored in a stone crock down in the springhouse. It's from a milch cow I've got in the corral out back. A family on their way to California traded her to me for fifty pounds of flour and ten pounds of chick-peas. That old cow sure does give sweet milk, Miss Sinclair," Scovill continued, a glint in his eye, "even though her disposition is as sour as vinegar, and do you know why it is?"

Julia, catching Cimarron's eye, smiled faintly. "No, Mr. Scovill, I have no idea why the cow you took in trade has such a sour disposition. Why does she, pray tell?"

"Well, it's like this. Those folks who traded her to me did so on account of how they were down on their luck. Their wagon capsized when they were fording the Canadian and they lost most of their provisions. Which is what forced them to trade their old Bossy to me for some supplies, like I said. Well, now, that there cow, she'd been counting on spending her remaining years just a-lounging around in the grass out in California, and when her plans went bust, why, she fell into a permanent sulk. But, like I said, that don't affect the sweetness of the milk she gives a'tall, which is, to my way of thinking, some kind of miracle."

"I would welcome a glass of cold milk, Mr. Scovill."

"Did you ever hear such a tall tale before?" asked an amused Julia of Cimarron after Scovill had hurried out of the room, promising to return as soon as he had gotten the requested cup of milk.

"Seth missed his calling in life," Cimarron remarked. "He should have been a storyteller. He's a bookish kind of man, as you can probably tell." He pointed to the books piled on the dirt floor next to the fireplace. "Seth loves books more than he does people," he told Julia. "He never had much schooling, he told me once, so he's pretty much a self-taught scholar."

"He lives here all alone?" Julia asked. "I mean, he has no wife?"

"Seth always claimed no woman would have a man as mean as he was, so he says he never tried to talk one into marrying him. He says he's got all the company he needs, what with folks stopping by here to rent a bed or buy a meal from him before moving on. But his real company is in those books over there. Men like Emerson and Washington Irving. He and them get along just fine I gather."

"What time will we be leaving in the morning?" Murdoch asked Cimarron.

"Midmorning ought to be soon enough, I reckon," Cimarron replied. "Or early afternoon if Miss Sinclair here turns out to be a late riser."

Murdoch's eyes landed on Julia. His brow knitted in a frown. "I truly mean no offense, Miss Sinclair," he intoned, "but I must state quite frankly that I would prefer to travel without you." Turning to Cimarron, he added, "Her wagon will only slow us down."

"Are you in some kind of a race to get to Wetumka, Murdoch?" Cimarron asked.

"May I remind you, Cimarron, that we have a business arrangement. I'm paying you good money to—"

"It's a business arrangement you can feel free to cancel out on at any time that strikes your fancy, Murdoch. Only if you do decide to do that, I want to warn you that I'm not turning back to you the hundred dollars you've already paid me. I figure I've already earned that."

Murdoch rose from the table and stormed out of the room, almost colliding with Scovill as their host returned carrying a cup of milk, which he placed in front of Julia.

She raised the cup to her lips and sipped from it. "It's delicious, Mr. Scovill. Just as sweet as a summer day."

"Told you so, didn't I?" Scovill crowed happily.

Later, as Cimarron and Julia rose from the table, Scovill offered to show them their accommodations. He took them to one end of the room and he drew back the canvas curtain to reveal a small square room with a number of bunks along its walls. "The men sleep in here," he declared, and then led them to the opposite end of the room and drew back the other canvas curtain. "In here's the women's quarters. I know it's not near good enough for a fine lady such as you appear to be, Miss Sinclair, but I hope you can put up with it for the one night you'll be here."

"I'm sure it will be fine, Mr. Scovill," Julia said graciously.

"How'd you like to take the evening air?" Cimarron asked her. "We could go for a stroll if you want to."

"That would be nice."

Cimarron, ignoring the wicked wink Scovill gave him when Julia's back was turned, escorted her outside.

"It's rather chilly, isn't it?" she asked as they walked out onto the open plain.

Cimarron started to take off his buckskin jacket.

"Oh, you mustn't," she protested. "I have a shawl in my carpetbag. It's in the wagon. I'll get it."

When she returned to him, they walked on as the stars began to appear in the sky and the moon began to rise, neither of them saying anything until Cimarron finally broke the silence with "It'll be a pleasure traveling with you all the way to Wetumka."

"It's nice of you to say so. But I may not be going to Wetumka after all."

Cimarron wondered if the disappointment he was feeling showed on his face. "You've changed your mind about making the trip?"

"Well, no, not exactly. I—it's just that I'm no longer quite so certain of my plans."

"I know it's none of my business, but is it a case of you getting cold feet about traveling on to Wetumka on account of what happened when your team spooked?"

"No, it isn't that."

"Miss Sinclair—"

"Why don't you call me Julia? There's really no need for such formality between us, is there?"

"Julia," he repeated, encouraged by her suggestion; he viewed it as close to a kind of invitation that he was eager to accept. "Julia's a real pretty name—as pretty as the one it belongs to."

Julia smiled. "You flatter me, Cimarron."

"Didn't mean to. I just told you the truth."

"There you go again."

Encouraged still further by the bright blaze of her smile, he took a step toward her. She took a step away from him. He reached for her. She eluded his grasp and started walking back to the road ranch. He quickly caught up with her.

"What's your hurry?" he asked her as she sharply increased her pace.

"I know I am in your debt, Cimarron. But I really think it's unfair of you to try to take advantage of me because of that fact."

"Julia, I wasn't trying to take advantage of you. I was just trying to—"

"Hush! I know what you were trying to do, and I think it was contemptible of you to act the way you did."

He took her arm in an attempt to halt her. She surprised him by turning sharply toward him and slapping his face, causing him to release his hold on her. He watched as she went running toward the road ranch and he shook his head in chagrin as she disappeared inside the building.

"No luck, I gather, with the little lady?"

Cimarron turned to find Murdoch moving through the darkness toward him. Ignoring the man's pointed remark, he said, "We'd best stand watch tonight in case Tolliver and Atkins should show up and try to ambush us in our beds."

"You think they will?"

"I think they might. I'll take the first watch. Relieve me at midnight." Cimarron strode away, his hand resting on the butt of his .44, and for the next several hours he patrolled the perimeter of the road ranch, keeping well away from the cleared area of land on which it sat and making his silent and alert way through the surrounding trees.

He saw no one and heard nothing that was not a sound made by some harmless night creature. By the time the position of the polestar indicated that midnight had arrived, he had almost come to the conclusion that his sentry duty had been a waste of time. He considered not bothering to wake Murdoch. But as he made his way back to the road ranch, he changed his mind. Just because neither Tolliver nor Atkins had put in an appearance during his tour of duty, he reasoned, didn't mean that they might not yet show up before the night was over.

He entered the ranch and made his way slowly through the darkness until he reached the hanging canvas that separated the men's sleeping area from the main room of the ranch and ducked under it. The moonlight streaming through the one uncurtained window enabled him to make out Murdoch and Scovill sleeping in bunks on opposite sides of the room. He went over to Murdoch and shook him.

Murdoch spluttered, mumbled something, and then swung his legs over the side of his bunk. He scratched himself, yawned, pulled on his shirt and pants and then his boots. "Anything happen?" he asked sleepily as he got to his feet.

"Nothing. But that don't mean you shouldn't keep a sharp eye out."

Murdoch ducked under the canvas, and a moment later Cimarron heard the door open and then close.

He sat down on one of the bunks as Scovill, in the bunk on the opposite wall, began to mutter in his sleep. Cimarron, his left boot gripped in both hands, remained motionless for a moment, thinking.

I don't need sleep, he told himself, near as much as I need what I could get from a woman like Julia Sinclair if she were in a giving mood. He lowered his booted foot to the dirt floor. He glanced at the swaying canvas. She's so close I can almost hear her breathing, he thought.

He stood up. And then he sat back down again. He lay down on the bunk and clasped his hands behind his head. She wants no part of you, he advised himself. So stay put and forget about her. He closed his eyes. But he couldn't sleep. Images of Julia Sinclair cavorted in his mind. She beckoned to him, gave him a seductive smile. He opened his eyes and she was still there dancing and prancing about in the thick darkness, daring him to try to take her.

I ought to explain to her about what happened between us before, he thought. Maybe if I could just make her understand that I wasn't trying to take advantage of her as she seemed to think I was trying to do—maybe then she and me, we could . . .

He practically leapt out of the bunk. There was a smile on his face as he made his way to the canvas, ducked under it, and started for the other canvas on the far side of the room. In his lusty hurry, he bumped his knee against a chair and then almost fell over the books piled on the floor by the fireplace. When he finally did reach the canvas, he halted and softly spoke her name. When she didn't answer, he spoke her name more loudly. Then, when he still received no response, he pulled the canvas aside and squinted into the deep darkness. Since there was no window in the room, he could see absolutely nothing. Nor could he hear anything. He began to grope his way along the wall, feeling his way from bunk to bunk, checking to see if they were occupied. At the end of the room, he crossed over and made his way back along the opposite wall, feeling the pallets of each of the bunks he came to and finding them all empty.

Where was she? he wondered. I didn't hear her leave the building. But maybe she'd gone out before I got back here. He rejected that idea because he was sure, if that was indeed what she had done, he'd have seen her out in the open.

He pulled the canvas aside, and as it dropped down behind him, he saw the door that was open a crack, admitting a narrow shaft of moonlight.

He remembered hearing the door close behind Murdoch. He had not heard it open again. He went to it and, opening it wider, peered out into the night.

He saw nothing at first but then a thick shadow detached itself from all the other shadows and he realized he was staring at Murdoch and Julia as they stood close together in the night, their arms wrapped around each other, their lips pressed tightly together.

He knew at once what had happened. Julia had been waiting for her chance at Murdoch. She had probably been awake when Murdoch left to stand his watch, and had followed him, carefully opening the door so that it would make no sound and then not bothering to close it so that no one would detect her departure.

Cimarron swore, damning both Murdoch and Julia. Murdoch because the man was in a position where he could easily be murdered if Tolliver and Atkins were anywhere in the immediate vicinity; Julia for preferring Murdoch to him. He resisted the impulse to angrily slam the door. Instead, he left it exactly as he had found it and started back to bed.

On the way he stopped, remembering Scovill's books. He felt his way about until he came upon them. He took a wooden match from one of the rolled-up legs of his jeans, used his fingernail to light it, and then began to examine the books. He was on his third match when he came upon a volume of Edgar Allan Poe's collected stories. He picked it up, blew out the match, and made his way back to his bunk.

Reaching it, he lit the stump of a candle that sat in an iron wall bracket, and lay down. He opened the book and scanned its table of contents. He turned to the opening page of "The Fall of the House of Usher" and began to read.

During the whole of a dull, dark, and soundless day in the autumn of the year, when the clouds hung oppressively low in the heavens, I had been passing alone, on horseback, through a singularly dreary tract of country, and at length found myself, as the shades of evening drew on, within view of the melancholy House of Usher. I know not how it was . . .

Cimarron looked up at the closed window when he heard the faint nicker of a horse, then, when all was silent again, he continued to read.

. . . but, with the first glimpse of the building, a sense of insufferable gloom pervaded my spirit. I say insufferable . . .

He closed the book when he realized he had been barely aware of what he was reading; a stark vision of the entwined bodies of Julia and Murdoch blazed in his mind. Why Murdoch, he wondered, and not me? He sure is a lucky bastard to have her after him. He—

The sudden sound of many horses' hooves pounding the ground outside caused Cimarron to leap from his bunk and run to the window. He could see nothing but the limbs of trees swaying in the windy night. He left the bunk area, went through the main room of the road ranch and then outside. Murdoch, he saw at once, had vanished. So had Julia. So had all the horses.

What the hell? Cimarron stared at Julia's repaired wagon, which stood horseless next to the corral. Where the hell was she? And where was Murdoch? Did they run off together? But if that's what they did, where are the rest of the horses? They only needed two. I'm going to have a long walk ahead of me without my black no matter which direction I set out in, he thought. He turned, heading for the road ranch. But he never reached the door. The sound of a man softly calling his name halted him in his tracks and caused his hand to drop to the butt of his Colt. He swiftly turned in the direction from which the sound had come, but he could see no one.

"Cim-a-rron."

Murdoch, he thought. That's Murdoch who's calling me, and he sounds like he can hardly talk. He made his way toward the spot where he had seen Murdoch and Julia embracing, his .44 out of its oiled holster now and held firmly in his right hand.

"Murdoch, where are you?"

"Here."

Cimarron turned to the right and saw Murdoch lying on the ground at the base of a tree, a shapeless mass that might have been merely a low pile of underbrush. He hunkered down beside the man, whose eyes were closed.

"Is it you?" Murdoch asked in a weak voice, holding

his left hand, which clutched a short and bloody-bladed knife, over the wound in his chest.

"It's me. Who the hell knifed you? Was it Tolliver? Atkins?" Cimarron looked up and around him, trying to penetrate the darkness in case it harbored unfriendly men with guns.

"No," Murdoch murmured faintly.

"No what?"

"Not them."

"Not Tolliver and Atkins. Then who?"

"Her."

"Julia Sinclair knifed you?"

Murdoch managed a nod. "I got the knife away from her. Was going to—wanted to—use it on her."

"Goddamn it to hell," Cimarron muttered. "She ran off, but before she did, she let loose our horses—and Scovill's too—so we couldn't come after her right away. I'll have to go hunting those horses come first light. Murdoch, why'd she do it? Did you insult her modesty?"

Murdoch shook his head. "She came out and she started to—to make up to me. I was the most surprised man in the whole world. But I let her have her way. Why not? Who wouldn't have? And then she knifed me. I fought with her, got the knife away from her. She ran. I told her I was going to kill her. And then I passed out."

"You've still not told me why she knifed you."

"She told me"—Murdoch's breath whistled wetly through his teeth—"she was Al Tolliver's fiancée."

"You didn't know her?"

"Never saw her before yesterday. She told me that Bill Tolliver, after our fracas in Fort Smith, went to his Uncle Obadiah Hoyt's farm in Arkansas, where she happened to be visiting, and told him what had happened. Said he was going to round up Dusty Atkins and come after you and me just as the pair of them did later on. Julia wanted to ride with them. Said she wanted to kill me to get revenge for me having brought Al Tolliver in so the law could hang him. She intended to kill you too, she said, if she had to to get to me. But

86

Tolliver wouldn't let her come with him. So, she said, soon after Tolliver left, she set out on her own. When she got to Fort Smith, she asked around about us and found out where we were headed from the man who runs the livery there.

"She must have passed us when we detoured to the north back there along the trail. And then . . ." Murdoch began to cough and it was more than a minute before he could continue speaking. "And then she had that trouble with her team and we just happened to catch up with her, and well, you know the rest."

"I know it and I like none of it. I'll give you a hand back to the ranch and we'll see what we can do for that wound of yours."

"It's a deep one," a sleepy-eyed Scovill said as he peered down at the knife wound in Murdoch's chest.

A shirtless Murdoch, lying on his back on the table, swore. "First I have a bullet in my arm and now a knife in my chest. Those friends and folk of Al Tolliver are killing me in pieces."

Kneeling in front of the fireplace, Cimarron used a bellows to fan the fire into bright-red life. He rose and hung the kettle, which Scovill had filled earlier at the spring, on the smoke-charred hook above the fire. Then he rose and went over to the table to stare down at Murdoch. "It's lucky that lady's knife didn't bite any deeper than it did, or you might be dead by now."

"The blade hit one of my ribs," Murdoch said. "If it hadn't, it might have gone clean through a lung and, you're right, I'd be out of commission for good."

When the water was boiling, Cimarron poured some into a porcelain pan Scovill had given him. Using some clean rags soaked in hot water, he swabbed Murdoch's wound.

Murdoch flinched and then began to bite his lower lip to keep from crying out. "Go easy, can't you?"

"Got to clean out this hole you got in you real good so it don't get infected." Cimarron continued cleaning the wound, causing blood to flow anew.

Murdoch uttered a string of obscenities and then clamped his jaw and his eyes shut as he gripped the sides of the table with both white-knuckled hands.

Ten minutes later, his ordeal ended, he sat up and swung his legs over the side of the table. "I feel kind of woozy," he said, looking down at the clean rag that covered his wound and was held in place by another thin strip of cloth tied around his chest. "What the hell do I do now?" he asked rhetorically. "I can't stay here, for that Sinclair woman knows who I am. Damn her, she might come back to finish the job she started with that knife of hers."

"That brings up something I've been intending to talk to you about," Cimarron said to Murdoch. "Julia knows you're here. She also knows you and me are on our way to Wetumka, as she claimed she was. By the way, Murdoch, she told me last night that she might not be going to Wetumka after all, which surprised me at the time. But now we know why she said what she did to me."

Murdoch snorted angrily. "Because she was after me and she figured she could do the job right here without traipsing all the way to Wetumka with us."

"That's right. But, as I was saying, she knows too much about us and our plans. Now Tolliver and Atkins, they don't know where we are at the moment, but they do know, the same as Julia does, that we're heading for Wetumka. What I'm getting at is maybe you ought to consider changing your plans under the circumstances. Go somewheres else besides Wetumka is what I mean."

Murdoch shook his head and tucked his shirttail into his pants. "I'll not be deterred by those three. I'm going to Wetumka. I've got important business to see to there. Very important business. And as for you"—he stabbed a finger at Cimarron—"you are being paid to keep those would be killers away from me and me in one piece. It does seem to me that you've been falling down on both jobs, and that makes me think two things: one is that I may be wasting the money I already paid you, and the second one is maybe I should start traveling on my own."

"I admit what you say is true. I reckon it's up to you to decide if you want to stick with me or try to make it to Wetumka on your own."

Murdoch frowned and shook his head in disgust. "Here I am with three manhunters on my trail and the former deputy marshal I hired to protect me can't seem to keep their bullets and knives from tearing me to pieces."

Cimarron remained silent as Murdoch climbed down from the table. Scovill carried the blood-soaked rags and pan full of bloody water outside to dispose of them.

Murdoch made his way to the men's sleeping area. Cimarron stepped outside and beckoned to Scovill. When the man came over to him, he said, "I'll pay you ten dollars, Seth, to stand watch over that bounty hunter inside until I get back."

"Where you going?"

"To look for the horses." Cimarron pulled the folded bills Murdoch had paid him from his pocket, peeled off two fives, and handed them to Scovill. "There's two men after Murdoch along with Julia Sinclair." Cimarron described Bill Tolliver and Dusty Atkins to Scovill. "So look sharp, Scovill."

"I'll do that."

Cimarron went outside and examined the ground for sign. Then he moved out, following the trail the horses—and Julia Sinclair—had taken.

6

The trail he was following was plain in the bright moonlight, and he was pleased to see that all the horses had stayed together. He had followed it for more than two miles when he saw that one of the horses had turned sharply and headed north.

He stopped and studied the ground on his right and just ahead of him. He quickly came to the conclusion that it was Julia who was heading north, because the hoof prints on that trail dug deeper into the ground than did those of the other four horses. He hesitated, considering his next move. He could go after Julia—and the horse she was riding, which might turn out to be his black. Or he could continue trailing the other horses in hopes of catching all of them. What it all boils down to, he thought, is, do I go after a woman who attempted murder and the horse she's riding or do I go after the other horses? He made his decision and walked on at a brisk pace, following the trail of the horses which soon began to shift to the south. He thought as he walked that he and Murdoch would both need horses for their journey to Wetumka, and if he went after Julia, the most he could hope to gain would be a single horse—if he was able to catch up with her, which in itself was decidedly doubtful. She would, he knew, be anxious to put as much ground as possible between herself and any pursuer, and that would tip the odds in favor of her escaping from him.

He walked on, and as he came out of a wood over an hour later, he was elated to see a small herd of six horses—his black which he now realized he had forgotten to unsaddle, his pack horse, Julia's surviving horse, and Scovill's three—grazing in a bowl-like clearing just below the fringe of the forest behind him. He made his way down into the miniature valley, and as he did so, one of Scovill's horses lifted its head and stared at him for a moment before beginning to graze again. His black nickered as he approached it. When he reached it, he patted its neck and spoke soft words to it, told it he was real glad the two of them were together again, told it he thought it was high time the two of them were making tracks.

The black's glossy hide rippled under his gentle touch, and when he swung into the saddle, the horse tossed its head and began to circle. "We're taking your friends back with us," he told his horse, and then proceeded to herd the other five animals back the way he had come. It was slow going through the woods, but they finally emerged from it onto the high plain.

An hour later, he spotted a moonlit rider heading toward him from the north. A full five minutes later, when the rider had come much closer to him, he realized it was Julia Sinclair, her skirts hiked high on her legs, astride Murdoch's buckskin. Well, I'll be damned, he thought as she stood up in her stirrups and began to signal him. He drew rein and waited for her to join him.

When she did, neither of them spoke for a moment. Then, boldly meeting Cimarron's appraising gaze, Julia said, "I came back this way in the hope of finding you. I thought you might come looking for the horses— and me."

Cimarron waited for her to continue. When she didn't, he asked, "Why were you hoping to find me? To try killing me like you did Murdoch?"

She didn't flinch in the face of his accusation, nor did

she avert her gaze. "No, I didn't come back to try to kill you. I came looking for you because I wanted to make you an offer."

"An offer? What kind of an offer do you happen to have in mind?"

"When we were having supper at Mr. Scovill's road ranch last night, you and Murdoch at one point discussed the fact that he was paying you to travel to Wetumka with him. I assumed he was paying you to protect him from people like me who want him dead. Am I correct?"

"You are."

"How much is he paying you for that task?"

"Two hundred dollars. He's already paid me half, and I get to collect the other half once I get him safe and sound to Wetumka. But I'm still waiting to hear what kind of an offer it is you want to make me, and for what."

"I'm prepared to pay you five hundred dollars to help me kill Murdoch."

Cimarron whistled through his teeth and tilted his hat back on his head as he stared in surprise at Julia.

"That's more than twice as much as Murdoch's paying you to help him stay alive," she pointed out.

"I know that. I can't fault your offer for being niggardly, but I'm not for hire."

"Murdoch hired you."

"That's true. What I meant was, my gun's not for hire when cold-blooded murder's what I'm being hired to do."

Julia's features tightened and she looked off into the distance. "You didn't know Al Tolliver."

Cimarron, wondering about the sudden turn in the conversation, said, "Nope, I didn't. But Murdoch told me you told him that you and Tolliver were pledged to each other."

"He was a wonderful man, Al was."

"He was also a bank robber, according to Murdoch."

Julia looked back at Cimarron, her eyes boring into his. "Yes, he was," she responded defiantly. "But I didn't care. I loved him, and what he was or what he did made not the slightest bit of difference to me. Oh, I'll admit that I would have preferred that he weren't an outlaw. And yet ..." She paused for a moment. "Perhaps that isn't altogether true. The fact that Al was an outlaw—sometimes I think that was one of the things that made him seem to me to be a rather romantic figure, above and beyond the wonderful reality of his tenderness and gentle way with me.

"You look surprised, Cimarron. But don't doubt for a minute that Al Tolliver could be gentle and tender. I'm telling you the truth. My life was dull and colorless before I met him. Afterward, it seemed that everywhere I looked there were sunshine and rainbows. Al could do that, make that kind of miracle happen. He could change a person's life. He changed mine. He had such a wonderful laugh. There was a dimple in his chin, and when he laughed, it deepened and his eyes twinkled."

"It sure does sound like you loved him a whole lot."

A shadow seemed to pass over Julia's face. "Loved him? I adored him. I worshipped him and the very ground he walked on. His touch—it set me on fire. He had only to look at me and a feeling of warmth and security would sweep over me. When I was with Al, I was never afraid, never insecure. He was the kind of man who could banish a woman's fears completely, make her feel safe. Oh, how very desperately I loved him!"

Cimarron, watching Julia, saw her expression suddenly harden. When she spoke again, her voice, which had grown soft and almost caressing as she spoke of her love for Al Tolliver, was sharp and harsh. "But then Murdoch invaded our world, Al's and mine. Like some baleful force he overturned our world, put out its sun, and brought death and destruction where before his advent there had been only love and desire. When they hanged Al shortly after Murdoch brought him in, a part of me died too, Cimarron. Can you understand that? Can you comprehend what I'm saying to you?"

Without waiting for him to answer, Julia hurried on. "I attended the hanging. So did Murdoch, who didn't, of course, know me. I was almost as much a star attraction at that ugly event as was my poor Al himself. People who did know me kept looking at me, whispering about me. I think they wanted me to make a scene—to weep, to scream perhaps. I wouldn't give them the satisfaction of doing so. When the trap fell and Al was torn from this life in such an awful manner, I went home and at home I stayed for more than a week.

"I wept then, alone in my house with my loss. I wept bitter tears as I grieved for what had been and would be no more, and I vowed vengeance. I vowed that someday somehow I would find a way to get even with Murdoch for what he had done to me by apprehending Al. It was that vow that kept me alive during that terrible time. However, in the back of my mind, I didn't really think I would ever have a chance to do anything about it, but it was good to cherish my vow like some secret treasure that was worth a fortune to me.

"Then I happened to be visiting Uncle Obadiah Hoyt's ranch and Bill arrived there. He told Obadiah and me about having finally found Murdoch in Fort Smith. He'd been out hunting the man ever since the hanging of his brother. He told us about the shoot-out in Fort Smith that involved you. He said he was going to ask Dusty Atkins, who was a man who rode with Bill—"

"I know about Atkins. Him and Tolliver caught up with Murdoch and me. We flung some lead each other's way."

"I didn't know that. I'm glad they didn't succeed in killing Murdoch. I wanted—and still want—that pleasure for myself. But, as I was saying—"

"Murdoch told me what you told him you decided to do, about how you set out after him on your own."

"And met the two of you almost by accident yesterday when my team bolted." Julia moved the buckskin closer to Cimarron. "Five hundred dollars is a lot of money," she whispered to him.

"There's no denying that."

"You'll take it?"

"I'll not."

Julia stiffened and stared at him. "Why not?"

"To tell you the truth, I don't rightly know why not. All I know is that I can't make myself murder a man in cold blood. Though I'm no stranger to killing, I am a stranger to that kind of killing—the kind you're asking me to do."

"Six hundred."

Cimarron shook his head.

Fury flashed momentarily in Julia's eyes and then was replaced by a seductive glow. "Last night—you wanted me. I know you did."

Cimarron remained silent.

"If I give myself to you—here, now . . ."

Desire, a hot flood, surged up in Cimarron.

"If money won't buy your services, perhaps sex can." Julia leaned toward Cimarron and placed one hand on his, which were folded about his saddle horn.

He wanted to seize her, take her in his arms, press his lips against hers . . .

"We could go over there," she whispered to him, indicating with a nod of her head a small grove of loblolly pines that provided the only shelter visible on the plain. She kneed her horse and walked it toward the trees, glancing over her shoulder to see if Cimarron was following her.

He moved his black out after her and soon caught up with her. Neither of them spoke. The only audible sound was the keening sound of the wind as it swept through the branches of the pines.

Once inside the grove, Julia dismounted and turned to Cimarron, who was sitting his saddle and staring down at her. She held up her arms to him, her gesture both a plea and an enticement.

He slid out of the saddle and went to her. As they embraced, his shaft sprang into erect life. She was motionless in his arms at first, but then, as his tongue slid between her teeth, she began to writhe and her hands began to slide up and down his back.

"You won't be sorry you accepted my offer, Cimarron," she whispered huskily when their lips parted. Her tongue invaded his left ear. "Rather, you'll be very glad you accepted it. Al always told me I was the best in bed—better than any of the whores he could never seem to stay away from."

Cimarron gently fondled her breasts. "I'm surprised you stuck with him if he went with whores like you just said he was wont to do."

"I took it philosophically. It was either that or lose him. I was smart enough to be able to see that there was no changing him. You've heard the expression about a half-loaf being better than none? Well, I can tell you that Al's half-loaf was better by far than most other men's whole loaves."

Cimarron's hands fell away from her as Julia stepped back and began to unbutton her jacket. She slipped out of it and shivered. She was about to drop her skirt when she was seized by a violent bout of shivering.

"Put your clothes back on," Cimarron told her, "before you freeze to death."

"But I promised to—"

"Some other time." He watched her hurriedly put her jacket back on. He was about to turn and board his black when she came up to him, her left hand caressing the side of his face, her right hand deftly unbuttoning his fly.

She reached into his pants and got a grip on his shaft. And then, as she slid it out of his jeans, she suggested that he would be more comfortable if he sat down.

He did, his back braced against a pine, and she got down on her knees in front of him. She moistened her lips and then bent down and took him.

Cimarron closed his eyes. His hands, palms down, pressed against the ground while within him the fire that Julia had kindled began to burn brightly, sending heat through every cell in his body.

"Oh, honey," he sighed as the sucking sounds she

was making blended with the moans the rising wind was whipping from the pine trees' swaying branches.

Her head rose and fell, rose and fell. Cimarron, the fire within him now a conflagration completely out of control, thrust upward, impaling Julia, who merely continued her arousing rhythm.

His legs began to tremble and his toes began to curl as he felt himself getting ready to explode. Then he was erupting in a swift series of hot spurts and Julia's hands were doing wonderful things to him while he could only moan and gradually return to earth from which her expert ministrations had sent him happily soaring.

She straightened up and looked at him. "Good?"

"It was that," he said softly as he opened his eyes and met her gaze. "I can't for the life of me understand why Al Tolliver would have wanted whores when he had you."

Julia shrugged, dismissing his speculation and saying only, "Al traveled a lot in his profession, and he always had a strong need for women, so he simply took them where he found them. You strike me as a man made of the same mold."

"I reckon you're right about that." Cimarron buttoned his fly and rose when Julia did. As they made their way to their horses, he said, "It's time I was taking you back to Scovill's road ranch."

"Is that where Murdoch is?"

"He's there, all right."

"You're going to help me kill him when we get there?"

"Nope."

"Then why—what—"

"I'm going to leave you there with Scovill to stand guard over you so you won't cause Murdoch and me any more trouble."

"Leave me there?" Julia cried indignantly. "A prisoner? After the bargain we just made? After what I just did for you to fulfill my part of our bargain?"

"If you'll think back, honey, you'll maybe recall that I

didn't make any bargain with you. You talked. I only listened to what you had to say."

"Damn you!" Julia screamed, and made a lunge for his holstered Colt.

He stepped deftly out of her way, grabbed her arm, and forced her aboard Murdoch's buckskin. "You ride ahead of me so I can keep an eye on you," he ordered her.

"You'll be sorry for this, Cimarron. I promise you that. You'll rue the day you treated me in this fashion."

He swung into the saddle and herded the other horses after Julia as she rode east. When she suddenly and savagely kneed the buckskin into a wild gallop, Cimarron swore and took the rope that hung from his saddle horn. He fastened a wide loop and threw it. It settled neatly around the buckskin's neck, bringing the horse to a dust-stirring halt.

As Julia glared speechlessly at him, he rode out, leading the buckskin by the rope and driving the other horses he had found before him.

The remainder of their journey back to the Scovill road ranch was uneventful. Just as the ranch came into view in the first gray light of the coming day, a shot rang out. Cimarron drew rein and sat his saddle, listening and alertly scanning the area on all sides and directly in front of him. His hand dropped to his Colt as the door of the outhouse flew open and Scovill came scurrying out of the building surrounded by a swarm of flies. Frantically pulling up his pants, he headed for the ranch.

Before he reached it, its front door flew open and a woman came running out of the building. Scovill halted at the sight of her. He backed up several steps when Murdoch suddenly appeared in the doorway, a six-gun that was not his own in his hand. He took aim at the woman, who was emitting sharp cries of fear as she fled. Cimarron drew his .44 and put a bullet into the wall of the ranch halfway between Scovill and Murdoch. Both men turned to stare at him, expressions of surprise on their faces. He put his heels to his horse and headed toward the ranch, driving the other horses ahead of him. Partway, he dropped his reins, shifted his gun to his left hand, and swerved slightly, scooping up the running woman and tossing her over his black's withers.

He drew rein when he reached the ranch, holstered his gun, and made no move to stop the woman he had captured as she slid down to the ground and then stood there glaring first at him and then at Murdoch.

She was a short square-faced woman with pendulous breasts, heavy hips, and only the hint of a waistline. Her hair was blond, almost white under the sun, and her eyes were a pale watery blue. There were crow's feet at the corners of her eyes and lines crisscrossing her broad forehead. She's no raving beauty, Cimarron thought, but she's not really ugly neither.

"Glad to see you back, Cimarron," Scovill said, breaking the silence.

"What's been going on here?"

"Another attempted murder," Murdoch declared in answer to Cimarron's question. "With me as the potential corpse all over again."

"That woman there do it?" Cimarron asked as he dismounted.

"She tried to shoot me with this gun of hers, but she missed and I was lucky enough to get the damned thing away from her."

"She came here a few hours ago, Cimarron," Scovill volunteered. "Said she'd been traveling with a band of emigrants headed for California who dumped her when she got sick. She finally found her way here, she said." Scovill moved away to corral the horses.

"A pack of lies obviously," Murdoch muttered.

"What's your name?" Cimarron asked the woman, who was staring sullenly up at him.

"Her name's Rhoda Ford."

All three men turned toward Julia, who had answered Cimarron's question as she got out of the saddle.

"I tried my damnedest, Julia." Rhoda said in a somewhat plaintive voice. "But he was too slick for me. And it looks from here like you had no better luck with the other one."

"Meaning me?" asked Cimarron.

"Meaning you, mister," Rhoda affirmed.

"When you ran off from here," Cimarron began, addressing Julia, "you went and hooked up with Rhoda. Now, stop me if and when and where I go wrong, but my guess is you two cooked up a plan. You, Julia, were to try to find and delay me long enough for Rhoda to get here to the ranch and kill Murdoch. Is that it? Did I miss the boat by much?"

"That, essentially, was our plan," Julia admitted. "We thought one of us should go after whoever came hunting the horses I ran off and the other one should come here to Scovill's in case Murdoch was still here. I thought there was a better than even chance that he would be, because I was sure I had wounded him rather badly."

"You did that all right, you bitch," Murdoch stormed at Julia.

"If I spotted you," a Julia unperturbed by Murdoch's outburst continued, "I intended to stall you long enough to keep you from getting back here and preventing Rhoda from carrying out the other part of our plan."

"Then the offer you made me, it wasn't a real one?"

"Oh, it was real enough. I thought of it shortly before I spotted you. And it still stands. Five hundred dollars if you'll kill Murdoch for me."

"She tried to hire you to murder me?" an incredulous Murdoch asked Cimarron.

Instead of answering the question, Cimarron directed his attention to Rhoda. "What's your stake in this?"

"Al Tolliver and I were good friends before that bastard"—she indicated Murdoch—"saw to it that Al stretched a rope."

"I knew Rhoda lived northwest of this ranch," Julia offered. "When I fled from here, I made my way to her place and we made our plans."

"Rhoda must be one of the west's working women," Cimarron observed.

"What makes you say a thing like that, Cimarron?" an obviously puzzled Murdoch inquired.

"On account of Julia told me that Al Tolliver had a strong tendency to take up with such ladies during his travels."

"Politics, they say, makes strange bedfellows," Julia remarked. "Well, so does the desire for revenge. Under ordinary circumstances, I would never—not in one million years—have ever gone to such a woman for help. But I knew from things Al had brazenly told me about her that they were friends. I needed help in the unresolved Murdoch matter. I thought Rhoda would be glad to give it to me."

"And I was, by Beelzebub," Rhoda exclaimed emphatically. Then, angrily to Julia, as if she had just realized what the woman had implied about her, "And you needn't play miss-high-and-mighty with me, Julia Sinclair. Al told me all about you and how you just about wore him out every chance you got without benefit of bell, book, and candle any more than him and me ever had."

"Seth, you got a lock on your tack-shed door?" Cimarron asked as the proprietor of the road ranch rejoined them.

"Sure, I have, Cimarron. A good strong padlock. Got the key right here in my pocket."

"Lock these two ladies up in that shed of yours."

"Lock them— Cimarron, that's no place for them. It's dirty and smelly—"

Cimarron pulled another ten dollars from his pocket and waved it in front of Scovill's nose, prompting the man to say, "But it's nice and dry on account of I put a new roof on the place only last September. Come along, ladies."

Julia began to protest loudly, and she was quickly joined by Rhoda. But Scovill, shushing them as he would two schoolchildren, soon had them silent and safely locked in his tack shed. He pocketed the key and made his way back to where Cimarron and Murdoch were waiting for him. "What do you want I should do with the pair of them, Cimarron? You can't store females in tack sheds indefinitely like you would turnips in root cellars. They won't keep. They'll spoil."

"Don't let them loose for a week," Cimarron instructed him. "That ought to give Murdoch and me plenty of time to get to Wetumka, at which point my duty's done and they're no longer a danger to me."

"Take this gun," Murdoch said, handing Scovill the revolver he had taken from Rhoda. "If either one of those women gives you any trouble, use it on them."

Scovill, a shocked expression on his face, reluctantly took the gun from Murdoch and thrust it into his waistband. Just then a small figure appeared in the doorway of the ranch and then stepped back out of sight.

"That was much too big to be a rat," Cimarron remarked, "and far too small to be a horse. What are you keeping inside that wasn't there when I left, Seth?"

"Oh, that! That was just a tad who showed up here well after midnight looking for some vittles and a place to rest his weary bones. He ain't but twelve. His name's Alonzo Hicks."

Followed by the other two men, Cimarron made his way into the ranch, where he found a towheaded boy standing just inside the door. The boy was thin, and the faded cotton shirt and jeans he wore reached neither his wrists nor his ankles. His shoes were badly scuffed and his trousers were held up by only one suspender; the other part of the pair was missing. His eyes were brown and bright as they stared up at Cimarron, who towered over him.

"I thought I told you to stay put," Murdoch said to him.

"I did, just like you said to do, Mr. Murdoch. But then things got so quiet outside and I got a bad case of curiosity that would have killed a whole lot more than a cat. So I went to the door and took a look, and I can tell you I was glad to see that things had settled down some and nobody had got themselves killed."

"Cimarron, this is Alonzo Hicks, who is on his way west, he told me," Murdoch said, and sat down at the table. "Alonzo, this man's name is Cimarron and he's my partner I told you about."

"Glad to meet you, sir." Alonzo held up a hand, which disappeared into Cimarron's. He shook it, trying to be gentle, but he apologized when Alonzo winced.

"Mr. Murdoch told me before Miss Ford started her ruckus that you used to be a deputy marshal, Cimarron."

"That's right, boy, I was."

"When I get my growth, I might consider deputying as a way of making a living. Do you need much of an education before you can start starpacking, Cimarron?"

Despite himself, Cimarron smiled. "Nope, you don't. All you need is a thick head and an even thicker hide." He turned to Murdoch. "We'd best be getting out of here."

"You boys don't want to leave without some grub inside yourselfs, do you?" Scovill asked, looking from one man to the other. "I can rustle you up some in two shakes of a lamb's tail. What do you say?"

"Go do it," Murdoch said. "While you're about making a meal, I'm going to try to catch forty winks."

Cimarron started for the door.

"Where are you going?" Murdoch asked him uneasily.

"The horses need seeing to. They've been run ragged tonight."

"I'll lend you a hand, Cimarron," Alonzo volunteered, and followed Cimarron out of the ranch and around to the corral.

"That your mule?" Cimarron asked as he entered the corral.

"Yes, sir. His name's Pegasus."

Cimarron halted. He turned to look down at Alonzo, who was running his hands over the black's strong shoulders.

"How'd you come up with a name like that?"

"I read about this horse that there was once. It had wings"—Alonzo spread his arms wide—"like this and it could fly through the sky with the best of the birds."

As Cimarron began to strip the gear from his black,

and the pack horse, Alonzo proceeded to do the same for Murdoch's buckskin.

"That's Prince," he said matter-of-factly as he unbuckled the buckskin's cinch and was almost brought down to the ground by the weight of Murdoch's saddle.

Cimarron looked in the direction Alonzo had indicated and saw the short-haired mongrel sitting just outside the corral, its tail thumping the ground in a steady dust-stirring rhythm.

"Prince, he's made himself real scarce since him and me and Pegasus got here. He was out hunting in the dark no doubt."

Cimarron asked Alonzo if he'd mind rounding up some rags from Scovill, which sent the boy scampering like a squirrel over the poles of the corral and racing toward the ranch. He returned minutes later with his hands full of pieces of clean muslin, which he and Cimarron then began to use to rub the three horses down.

They worked in silence for some time, then, "Is it true that, like Mr. Murdoch said, you're his bodyguard?" Alonzo asked.

"It's true."

"Miss Ford, before she tried to shoot Mr. Murdoch, let on he was a bounty hunter." When Cimarron said nothing, Alonzo asked, "Is that true too?"

Cimarron nodded and removed a bur from his black's glossy tail.

"Everything happened so fast inside before when Miss Ford threw down on Mr. Murdoch that I couldn't figure out what was going on. Still can't—not for sure. How come Miss Ford tried to kill Mr. Murdoch?"

"Miss Ford was a friend of a man named Al Tolliver that Murdoch trailed and trapped for the bounty there was on Tolliver's head. Tolliver was hanged and Miss Ford was unhappy about that, so she decided she was going to get even with Murdoch for turning her friend in to the law."

"And the other lady that was with you when you rode up before with Miss Ford? Who was she?"

"She was also a friend of Al Tolliver. More than just a friend. She was fixing to marry Tolliver."

Alonzo busied himself with the buckskin, his brow wrinkled, obviously deep in thought. "How come—"

"Whoa, boy! I reckon you've about used up your quota of questions." Cimarron glanced at Alonzo, saw the grin on the boy's face, grinned himself, and said, "Now it's my turn to ask a question or two of you. Where you headed?"

"Where am I . . . Oh, west."

"How come?"

"My ma caught cancer just after this past spring's planting was finished, and she was dead in less time than it takes to tell about it. Me and Pa carried on without her as best we could, but it was hard. Pa, you see, he missed her real bad. I used to hear him a-talking a blue streak to her when I was supposed to be asleep up in the loft. He would talk real soft and low and then he would cry. Like I said, he took her passing mighty hard. He pined a lot and it was the pining some said that weakened him so that I had him to bury before the first leaves fell this fall. Well, with both Ma and Pa gone, I didn't rightly know what to do with myself. Finally I up and sold the home place out from under myself and went westering, and here I am."

Cimarron, finished with his black, and the pack horse, leaned back against the corral poles, hooking a boot heel on one of them as he studied Alonzo, who was working hard at his task, his small hands moving swiftly but gently over the buckskin's body. In Alonzo, he saw himself—the boy he had once been, who had also once left a homeplace to move out into the world and whatever awaited him there. He felt a pang of sorrow and then a fleeting sense of loss for the time and the place and two people—his ma and pa—who were all lost to him now in the vanished years. He resisted the impulse to go over to Alonzo, pat the boy's shoulder, and tell him that everything was sure to turn out all right for him. Because, he knew, it very well might not. The West was a big place and a boy could falter and fall before he learned to make his way in it. And some falls could be fatal.

Alonzo turned and told Cimarron, "I got me a Colt Peacemaker that used to belong to Pa and I got me a small stake that ought to do me for a little while longer, so I figure I've got a pretty good chance of making it. I come from hardy stock."

Cimarron heard the firm note of pride ringing in Alonzo's voice as he made his last statement. "I've no doubt you will, boy. No doubt at all." Liar, he chided himself. And then he argued silently with himself whether it would have been better for him to have told Alonzo the truth about what perils might be lying in wait for him.

"You want this buckskin saddled and bridled now, Cimarron?"

"I do." As Alonzo went to work on Murdoch's mount, Cimarron put his gear back on the black and then the load on the pack horse.

When he and Alonzo had both finished their tasks and had started back to the road ranch, Cimarron pointed to the smoke coming from the building's stone chimney. "It's not rising," he observed. "See how it sort of slides down around the chimney? That means weather's on its way. That and those snow blossoms up there in the sky and the way the wind's shifting to the east."

"Snow blossoms?"

Cimarron pointed to the white clouds drifting in the dawn sky. "Folks say they look like flowers when they shape up like that. That bluish tinge they've got sets them apart from other clouds too. Those kind of clouds say snow's on its way. And the falling smoke's another sure sign of a storm coming."

"Then no doubt you and Mr. Murdoch will be staying on here till it blows over."

"I doubt that. Murdoch's got ants in his pants about wanting to get to Wetumka, and though he's been wounded, I'm willing to wager he'll want to move out, storm or no storm. Which is fine with me."

As they entered the road ranch, Cimarron asked Alonzo if he had a warm jacket.

"Yes, sir, that's mine hanging on that nail over there."

Cimarron glanced at the canvas jacket that had the butt of a Peacemaker protruding from one of its two pockets.

"Sit down, Cimarron," Scovill commanded from where he was hunkered down in front of the hearth. "Everything's near to ready. Coffee's hot and ready to pour."

Cimarron, as he sat down across from Murdoch, beckoned to Alonzo to join them, but the boy shook his head. "What's the matter, you're not hungry?"

"No, sir, I'm not."

Cimarron shrugged and began to eat the food on the plate that Scovill had just placed in front of him.

"But Prince might be hungry," Alonzo said. "I'd be obliged to you if you'd save any scraps you don't want so I could feed them to my dog."

Later, when Cimarron had finished eating, he held out his plate, on which remained the skins of boiled potatoes, half a corn muffin, and some charred pieces of fatback. Alonzo took it, thanked him, and hurried out of the room.

"Looks like snow," Cimarron told Murdoch. "You want to stay here or do you want to try to ride?"

"We'll ride. If we stay, those two women are liable to find a way out of that tack shed and murder us both in our sleep."

"I've got the horses ready."

As Murdoch settled their bill with Scovill, Cimarron left the building. He arrived outside just in time to see Alonzo stuff the last of the food he had given him into his mouth.

"I thought you weren't hungry," Cimarron stated bluntly.

"I wasn't. But it turns out neither was Prince, so I thought it'd be a sin to let this food go to waste, so I et it."

"Boy, you know what you are? What you are is a barefaced liar. You wanted that food for yourself all along, which makes me think you don't have enough money to pay your way at a place like this."

"I already paid for the meal I had when I got here," Alonzo argued. "It's just that I only got so much money and I don't know for sure how far I've got left to go. So I have to try to stretch my money out. I hunt and fish. I find some berries, though they're getting scarce now what with winter coming on. I sleep out in the open. But once in a while I get a hankering to put up at some place civilized like Mr. Scovill's. I didn't mean no harm by what I did."

"I know you didn't, and I wasn't accusing you of trying to harm anybody." Cimarron dug down into his pocket and came up with what was left of the hundred dollars Murdoch had paid him, from which he peeled a bill. "Here's ten dollars."

"I can't take charity."

"You damn well can and you damn well better or I'll thrash you within an inch of your life."

Alonzo, after a long moment of hesitation, took the money Cimarron was holding out to him.

"Alonzo, I was in the selfsame spot you're in right now once upon a fairly long ago time. There were helping hands held out to me back in those days, along with a few kicks like those men give a cur nobody wants. But it's mainly the helping hands I recollect. I never could pay most of those folks back because I was always moving on. That ten dollars I just donated to you sort of makes me feel I'm paying back the people who helped me out of tight spots when I wasn't much older or bigger than you are at the moment."

"I'm obliged to you, Cimarron."

Murdoch came out of the ranch and headed for the corral. Cimarron gave Alonzo a wave and then followed Murdoch as fat flakes of snow began to skitter down out of the sky, which had grown completely cloudy.

7

Cimarron and Murdoch rode southwest as the snow continued to fall.

"That's all we need," Murdoch grumbled, his shoulders hunched and his hat pulled down low on his forehead.

"Manhunters after me and now snow to show my tracks as plain as day to anyone who cares to take a look at the goddamned ground."

Cimarron said nothing as Murdoch glanced nervously over his shoulder as if he expected to see someone on their back trail.

They rode on at a steady pace as a shaft of sunlight broke through the clouds, and soon afterward the snow stopped. As they covered the next several miles, the sun did battle with the snow blossoms littering the sky, and shortly after it had reached its meridian, there was hardly a cloud to be seen. They made camp for the night soon after crossing the tracks of the Missouri, Kansas, and Texas Railroad south of Checotah.

"Maybe we should have forded the Canadian before we made camp," Murdoch speculated as if he were talking to himself. "Sometimes a river like the Canadian does funny things. It can fill up and flood overnight and then we'll have to go way the hell out of our way to get past it."

"Murdoch, you sure are a worrier, aren't you? You

always look on the dark side of life. The river's not going to flood. The snow's stopped. So smile, Murdoch, and have some coffee. Maybe it'll cheer you up." Cimarron passed the pot to his companion, who filled his cup and drank. But Murdoch's sour expression didn't change as he continued to stare gloomily into the flames of the campfire.

When they had eaten their supper and cleaned up after it, Cimarron wrapped himself in his blanket. Lying on top of his ground tarp, he placed his revolver at his side and cradled his head in his saddle, which he was using for a pillow. He lay on his back looking up at the pattern of stars, which was shredded from time to time by wispy clouds floating across the night sky. He glanced to the side and saw Murdoch standing watch near a cottonwood that grew some distance from the fire. He yawned. Stretched. Turned over on his side and, with his arms wrapped around his body and his knees drawn up, closed his eyes and let sleep seduce him.

A snuffling sound awoke him some time later. He opened both eyes, but he didn't move a muscle. His arms remained wrapped around his body as he listened. There it was again. A wild hog rooting? Or somebody who needed to blow his nose? Tolliver maybe? Atkins? Cimarron turned over slowly, barely disturbing the blanket that covered him, got his hand on his gun, and looked up at the sky. The polestar was obscured by clouds, as was the moon, so he couldn't tell what time it was. But it mustn't be midnight yet, he thought, or Murdoch would have woke me up to take my turn at sentry duty.

He turned toward the tree where he had last seen Murdoch. The man was sitting at its base, his arms hanging by his sides, his hands lying listlessly on the ground, his head cocked and resting on his shoulder.

Cimarron caught a brief glimpse of a figure darting through the thin light cast by the dying fire. It took refuge behind a tree on the side of the fire opposite Murdoch. He raised his Colt, cocked it, and waited for the intruder to show himself again. He scanned the surrounding area, wondering if there was only one or if there were more, and who they were. He wasn't about to start asking questions. He'd shoot first and then—if his target was still alive— he'd ask questions. He wanted to call out to Murdoch, shout to him to wake up and to take cover. But he didn't. If he did, the intruder in the camp might very well attack before Murdoch could get out of sight. And since the stealthy figure Cimarron had seen was moving in Murdoch's direction, a shout would force whoever it was into swift and probably deadly action.

Cimarron suddenly and impatiently threw off his blanket and got to his feet. He started circling around the campfire, his eyes on the tree behind which the figure had disappeared. He intended to come up on whoever it was from behind, so he made his slow and careful way toward his destination, making no noise, hardly daring to breathe.

His pent-up breath gusted out of his nostrils when again he heard the snuffling sound, much louder now. An instant later he saw a small shape come hurtling out of the darkness and then another slightly larger shape come bounding after it. It took him several seconds to realize what he was seeing—Alonzo Hicks' dog, Prince, in rapid pursuit of a mule-eared jackrabbit.

As the jack veered suddenly and sharply to the left to escape it, the dog bared its teeth and seemed to leap through the air, landing directly in front of the jack and causing it to come to an abrupt halt. Then, as the dog's jaws snapped and Prince lunged toward its prey, the rabbit turned and went bounding away into the embers of the dying fire before it could stop itself. It caused a shower of sparks to spray the area, and then its coat caught fire. An instant later, the rabbit's entire body was ablaze and it went flopping along the ground with Prince still stalking it.

Murdoch, aroused by the commotion, was struggling to his feet and raising the gun in his hand.

"Get down," Cimarron shouted to him. "Take cover!"

Murdoch gave him a startled look, glanced at the

charred body of the rabbit that now lay twisting limply on the ground with Prince slavering over it, and dived behind a nearby tree.

A shot tore a low-growing sucker from the trunk of the tree behind which Murdoch had taken cover.

Cimarron ran to the spot where he had seen the flash of fire, circled the tree, and seized the shadowy figure holding a Peacemaker.

"Let me go!"

Cimarron didn't let him go. He lifted him off the ground and held tightly to the wildly struggling Alonzo Hicks, holding the boy's back against his chest as Alonzo kicked at him and tried with one hand to break his grip.

"What the hell do you think you're doing, boy?" Cimarron bellowed.

"Leave me be," Alonzo cried, his struggles intensifying.

"Answer my question, dammit, or I'll take my belt to you."

Alonzo aimed his gun over his shoulder at Cimarron.

Cimarron promptly knocked it out of his hand before he could fire. Then, after clouting Alonzo on the top of the head, he picked up the fallen Peacemaker and thrust it into his waistband. The boy continued his struggle to free himself. Cimarron tightened his grip on the boy's body, forcing most of the air from Alonzo's lungs.

"What the hell's going on over there?" Murdoch yelled from behind the tree where he had taken cover.

"It's about over," Cimarron yelled back. "I've caught the felon who just tried to plug you."

He relaxed his grip on Alonzo. "I'm going to set you down on the ground. You're going to turn around and face me and you're going to tell me what the hell this is all about." He put Alonzo down and then let him go. When Alonzo merely stood stiffly with his back to Cimarron, Cimarron reached out and roughly turned the boy around. "Talk!"

"It's the kid," an amazed Murdoch exclaimed as he

joined Cimarron, his gun in his hand. "He was the one shot at me?"

"He was the one."

"Why you—" Murdoch raised his gunhand and was about to pistol-whip Alonzo when Cimarron reached up and caught his wrist.

"Let go of me," Murdoch roared. "I'll teach this snot-nose a lesson he'll not soon forget about why he shouldn't sneak around in the night trying to ambush people."

"Simmer down, Murdoch," Cimarron ordered. "Let's see if we can't find out what this is all about. Don't you want to know who or what put him up to trying to kill you?"

"Money."

The single word Alonzo had spoken in a clear voice gained him the attention of both men.

"Money?" Murdoch repeated as Cimarron released him.

"I saw you had a lot on you back at the Scovill place," Alonzo explained, addressing Murdoch. "I meant for me to have some of it—maybe even all of it. I rode Pegasus and caught up with you here. I left my mule in the woods and—"

"Why, you conniving bastard," Murdoch yelled, and again raised his gun.

Again Cimarron stopped him from striking the cowering Alonzo. "That ten dollars I gave you," he said to the boy. "I take it that wasn't enough for a greedy little sneak thief and bushwhacker like you."

Alonzo avoided meeting Cimarron's piercing gaze.

"You gave him ten dollars?" Murdoch asked, incredulity in his tone.

"He gave me a hand with the horses. He was in need."

"You're a poor judge of character, Cimarron," Murdoch taunted. "I'm beginning to think you'd be dumb—or sentimental—enough to take a viper to your breast."

This time when Murdoch made his move, Cimarron failed to stop him in time. The barrel of Murdoch's six-gun struck Alonzo on the right temple, spinning the boy around to one side and sending him sprawling to the ground. He lay there, blood seeping through the abraded skin already turning black and blue.

"God damn you, Murdoch," an outraged Cimarron shouted, ready to attack his companion. "What the hell did you do that for? He's just a kid, for Christ's sake!"

"He's just a kid, all right. A kid with killing on his mind as he sets out to rob innocent people." Murdoch snorted his disgust. "Let's get the hell out of here before he comes to and you decide you ought to sit around and wet-nurse him till the king of all headaches I've no doubt given him has gone away."

Without waiting for a response, Murdoch went to where the horses had been left for the night and began to saddle and bridle his buckskin.

Cimarron looked up from the prone form of Alonzo by his boots to where the boy's dog was bellied down on the ground gnawing hungrily at the charred carcass of the jack, which he held pinned beneath his two front paws near the now-dead fire. He gave Alonzo one last glance and then he rejoined Murdoch. Ten minutes later, they rode away from their campsite without looking back at the still-unconscious Alonzo and Prince, who had curled up by his small master's side and was sleeping the sleep of the sated.

"That kid must have started trailing us as soon as we left Scovill's road ranch," Murdoch remarked. "But we ought to be able to shake him."

"I told him when we were readying the horses that we were headed for Wetumka," Cimarron confessed.

"Shit."

"So the thing for us to do is put as much distance as we can in between him and us in case he turns out to be a determined cuss and comes after us again once he wakes up."

"I'm not running my horse ragged just to shake a cutpurse kid from my tail," Murdoch stated flatly. "If he's dumb enough to come after us again, well, this time I won't just hit him, I'll kill him."

Cimarron gave his companion a sidelong glance and saw the firm set of his jaw and the cold light in the man's brown eyes. He had no doubt that Murdoch had meant what he said. Nor did he have any doubt at all that Murdoch would do exactly as he had threatened to do: kill Alonzo Hicks if the boy was foolish enough to make a second try for his money.

"The kid just might be clever enough to outfox you," he warned Murdoch, "so we might be a whole lot better off doing what I suggested: ride hard and fast away from here."

Murdoch shook his head, and when Cimarron started to protest the man's decision, he held up a hand. Cimarron stayed silent. And wary. He gradually dropped back behind Murdoch as both men rode on, and looked back over his shoulder more than once as they continued their journey to Wetumka. But he could see little in the moonlight and the keening early winter wind hid the sounds that were a normal part of a plains night. Both factors made him decidedly uneasy.

At first light the following morning, Murdoch proposed that they stop for breakfast. Cimarron objected, arguing that they would be better off without breakfast but with more miles between them and anyone who might be trailing them.

"I hope you're not worried about that Hicks kid," Murdoch remarked in a mocking tone. "In case you are, forget it. I can take care of him. I'll guarantee you that. And as for the Sinclair and Ford women, they're locked up safe and sound back at Scovill's, so they no longer pose a problem for us."

"But Bill Tolliver and Dusty Atkins aren't locked up anywhere," Cimarron pointed out.

"Neither have we seen hide nor hair of either one of them," Murdoch pointed out in turn. "They could have caught up with us easily by now if they had wanted to. No, my guess is that they gave up the chase after we ran them off last time. Besides, I got Tolliver in the leg. Maybe he's dead by now from loss of blood or something. Anyway, I'm more hungry than I am afraid of anybody who might be after us."

"You're the boss," Cimarron declared somewhat reluctantly. He pointed to a stream glistening in the distance, both of its banks lined with cottonwoods. "We could build a fire in under those trees growing over there so our smoke'd get lost in their branches and would most likely not get to be seen by anybody. The trees would give us a natural kind of cover too."

"Let's go."

Cimarron followed Murdoch over to the stream and into the cluster of cottonwoods, where he dismounted and proceeded to build a fire, using wood he took from a dry deadfall.

By the time the sun had topped the rim of the canyon, sending its rays spilling down into it, they were finishing the last of the boiled rice and baked potatoes that Cimarron had cooked. Murdoch poured himself a second cup of coffee and sat cross-legged on a flat rock as he sipped it. Cimarron, his hat tilted back on his head and one leg propped across his other knee, leaned back against the trunk of a cottonwood and stared up at the campfire's smoke drifting among the trees' bare branches. He took a deep breath and then began to cough, as the light wind shifted, sending smoke flying into his nostrils.

He was still coughing and his eyes were watering badly when a male voice shouted, "Come out of there, the two of you, with your hands held high."

Instead of obeying the shouted order, Cimarron drew his gun and fired in the direction from which the shout had come. "On your feet, Murdoch," he yelled. "Let's get the hell out of here!"

Murdoch sprang to his feet, dropping his coffee cup, and ran toward his buckskin. He was about to board it when Cimarron's fire was returned—from three separate directions. Murdoch took cover behind his horse and began to shove it toward an area where the trees grew thickest.

Cimarron, some distance away, took cover behind a

tree and returned the fire. He waited a moment and then made a dash for the next nearest tree, on his way to his horse. Bullets halted his progress, some of them biting into the tree behind which he had taken cover.

"There are three of us this time, Murdoch."

Cimarron recognized the voice as Bill Tolliver's.

"And we mean to do for you and that damned deputy that's siding you this time for sure and certain."

Cimarron also recognized the second voice. It belonged to Dusty Atkins.

"You better pray, Murdoch," a third voice that was unfamiliar to Cimarron advised, a voice that was full of fury. "You'd best pray that one of us kills you; if you have the bad luck to be taken alive, you'll wish that we'd killed you ten times over, cuz we're going to see to it that you die real slow."

"That was my uncle, Obadiah Hoyt, talking, Murdoch," Tolliver called out. "We met him on the trail while we were hunting you. It seems he couldn't sit still and wait at home for us to do the job. He had to come after you himself to get even for what you did to his favorite nephew. And me, I also got a score to settle with you, Murdoch, for being the devilish instrument of my brother's hanging."

"We're three and you're only two," Atkins shouted. "So give up, Murdoch. Tell your partner it's time for you boys to throw in the towel."

Murdoch's answer to Atkins' suggestion was a shot, which silenced the three ambushers. It silenced them only momentarily. A sudden fusillade of rounds tore through the grove of cottonwoods.

During the loud volley, Cimarron made it to the next tree. And the next. He didn't return the fire, not wanting to announce his position or make himself a ready target for the three attackers. One more tree, he thought, his eyes upon it. He hesitated, listening to the ominous silence, then he ran for it. He made it, staying behind the tree for only a moment, then he was running again. He leapt aboard his black and yelled at the top of his voice, commanding Murdoch to follow him. As Murdoch climbed into his saddle, Cimarron emptied his .44 to cover the man's retreat. Then, as both men galloped out of the grove and onto the open plain, he pulled his Winchester from its boot. When, several minutes later, the three men rode out of the cottonwoods, he raised the weapon and fired at them.

They kept coming.

Cimarron turned and rode on, lashing his black with his reins and shouting to Murdoch, who had fallen slightly behind him, to hurry up. Five minutes later, Murdoch suddenly turned his horse and started riding north.

Now, where the hell does he think he's going? Cimarron wondered. He shouted Murdoch's name.

"This way," Murdoch yelled back to him, and pointed straight ahead of him to the mouth of a canyon that was not far away.

"No," Cimarron shouted, but Murdoch rode on. He swore, shouted again, and then realized that Murdoch was too far away now to hear his warning. He wanted to ride on, but he knew he couldn't. He had taken Murdoch's money. He had agreed to help Murdoch get safely to Wetumka. He couldn't desert the man now, even though he was riding straight into a trap in the form of a box canyon he knew well from the many times he had passed through this part of Indian Territory during his days as a deputy. He kneed his horse and went galloping after Murdoch, who was rapidly approaching the entrance to the box canyon. He turned in his saddle and fired at the three horsemen behind him. Then he was at the canyon's entrance, and a moment later he was inside the natural trap that Murdoch had also entered.

Just inside the mouth of the canyon, where a pile of boulders lay strewn haphazardly as if by giants' hands, both men hurriedly dismounted and took cover. Cimarron hastily reloaded his Colt and began to return the fire coming from outside the canyon, as did Murdoch.

He could see nobody, but he watched for flashes of gunfire before squeezing off a round in the hope of hitting one of the three well-hidden men. He knew they were bound and determined to see two corpses—his and Murdoch's—littering the floor of the canyon before they left the area.

He glanced over his shoulder at the stream of water spilling over the canyon's rear wall, part of it dissolving into a spray while the remainder splattered on the eroded surface of a huge rock resting on the canyon floor. He estimated that the lowest part of the canyon's wall was a good fifty feet above the ground.

A bullet slammed into the boulder he was crouching behind, sending stone-dust spraying into his face and forcing him to hunker down closer to the ground. He gripped his gun in both hands, propped its barrel on the boulder, and squeezed off a round. Beside him, Murdoch continued firing, cursing their attackers and the trap he had so unwittingly ridden into.

"I tried to stop you," Cimarron told him, his eyes on the narrow entrance to the canyon, his gun still propped on the boulder and aimed in that direction. "I know this place. I've passed it a few times. The only good thing about it is it's got water."

"How the hell are we going to get out of here alive?" Murdoch asked, and ducked as a bullet whined over his head.

"You'll never get out of there alive," Tolliver yelled as if in answer to Murdoch's question. "We three can stay out here till the cows come home—and until you two starve to death in there."

Murdoch spat an obscenity and fired a round.

"You'll run out of ammunition, you keep on shooting so much," Tolliver yelled. "Then the three of us can just mosey on in there and pluck you two like you were prairie chickens."

"He's right, dammit," Murdoch muttered. "We've got no food—we left our packhorse back in those cottonwoods where we made camp."

"Maybe they're bluffing," Cimarron speculated. "Maybe they've got no more food than we have."

"Even if that's true, they can at least send one of

their number out to hunt. What the hell are we going to hunt boxed up in here like we are? Ants?"

The standoff continued for another hour, punctuated with sporadic gunfire from both inside and outside the canyon. The sun topped the canyon wall and began to blaze down into it, causing heat waves to rise shimmering from its flat floor.

Cimarron made his way to where the stream plummeted over the top of the canyon wall. Taking off his hat, he partially filled it with water and drank. Then he refilled it and carred it back to Murdoch, who took it from him gratefully and quickly emptied it.

"I'm getting out of here," Cimarron announced as he clapped his wet hat back on his head.

Murdoch gave a skeptical snort. "Now, just how do you propose to do that? Fly out?"

"Climb out."

"Climb out?" Murdoch echoed. He turned and looked at the canyon walls surrounding them. He gave an aborted bark of laugh. "You'll never make it. A fly couldn't climb up there, for Christ's sake."

"You keep those fellows out there amused, will you, while I see what I can do about getting out of here. If I make it, I'll circle around—"

"And if you don't make it, you'll wind up as mincemeat on the canyon floor."

"—and come in behind those boys out there. Then we can catch them in our crossfire. How's that strike you?"

"It would be great if you could manage it." Murdoch tilted his head back and looked wistfully up at the rim of the canyon wall. "But —"

Cimarron never heard what Murdoch said because he was already striding toward the nearest sheer expanse of skyward-soaring rock. He holstered his gun, looked up to judge the distance, and then sprang upward. His outstretched fingers closed on a section of projecting rimrock. He swung there, holding tightly to the rock as his feet scrabbled for purchase on the side of the wall. He managed to hook his right foot over another slight projection. Hauling himself up, he reached higher with his right hand and gripped an outthrust slab of rock, while his left foot dug into the side of the wall and he pushed himself still higher.

His progress was slow, but it was progress. Like some huge insect, he crawled slowly up the face of the cliff, hand over hand, foot over foot, his fingers beginning to bleed as the skin was scraped from them by the wall's rough surface. Sweat slid down his forehead and ran into his eyes. He blinked the salty water away as he continued to climb. Suddenly he slipped and his feet swung out into the empty air and his heart lurched within his chest as he held on grimly, desperately with both hands.

Below him guns spoke in their deadly language, and he clearly understood what they were saying. If he and Murdoch failed to escape from the canyon, they would die here at the hands of the three men ouside it. He managed to get his feet positioned in a narrow crevice; then, after catching his breath, he looked up and promptly shut his eyes, because he found himself staring directly into the blinding face of the still-rising sun.

He climbed on, not looking up anymore at the seemingly unreachable rim that was his destination and not looking down at the canyon floor either, which receded slowly beneath him as he continued his determined climb. His shoulders began to ache. His fingers became slippery with blood. His arms were two tense masses of quivering muscle. The beat of the blood in his veins drummed in his head and his teeth ground audibly against one another.

He kept climbing. Another inch. Another foothold. One more handhold.

The floor of the canyon—so far below now. The rim of the canyon—still so far above him. He kept climbing, inch by agonizing inch. Occasionally, he tore loose frost-cracked rock that drifted down into his sweat-slicked face, almost blinding him. He kept climbing.

And then his groping left hand bent forward at the

wrist and he realized that he had finally reached the rim of the canyon. His breath rushed from his throat as he clawed at the canyon's rim with both hands while his feet scrambled for purchase on the rough wall. He braced himself and then heaved himself upward. A moment later, he was over the rim and lying panting on its flat surface, his feet dangling over its edge. He lay there, sucking air into his lungs, the right side of his face pressed against the sere grass, his heart's thunder causing his blood to pound through his brain and body.

He got his hands under him and was starting to push himself up from the ground when he heard the soft swish of footsteps in the grass. He looked up and saw skirts, raised his head even higher and saw the two women, both of them smiling down at him. He groaned and lowered his head. He looked up again and they were both still there. His eyes shifted from their smiling faces to the knife in Julia Sinclair's hand and the six-gun in Rhoda Ford's hand.

"How'd you two get here?" he asked them.

It was Julia who answered him. "When Scovill brought us food last night, Rhoda cozied up to him and I got behind him and brained him with a hammer I found in the tack shed he put us in."

"Then we took my gun away from him before he could regain consciousness," Rhoda added, "and the knife Julia had used to try to kill Murdoch and some gear. We put the gear on two of his horses and here we are!"

"Where's Murdoch?" Julia asked Cimarron in a deceptively silken voice.

"Down below," he answered, and got to his feet, every muscle in his body protesting the effort.

"In the canyon?"

He nodded.

"Take a look, Rhoda. He could be lying to us."

"I wouldn't put it past him." Rhoda circled around Cimarron, keeping him under her gun, and peered down into the canyon. "He's down there," she confirmed.

"Shoot him."

"He's out of range." Rhoda frowned. "We'll never get him now. We can't climb down there from here. And the men down below are sure to get him sooner or later."

"Hush! Let me think." Julia was silent for several minutes. Then, "We'll take Cimarron down to the mouth of the canyon and offer to turn him over to Bill Tolliver and the others. Then we'll—" Julia fell silent and beckoned to Rhoda, who rejoined her. The two women whispered together for several minutes while Rhoda kept her gun trained on Cimarron.

"Drop your gun," Julia ordered him. "And that other gun you've got in your waistband."

Reluctantly, Cimarron did as he was told. Rhoda retrieved his .44 and Alonzo's revolver which had been in his waistband. She handed his .44 to Julia and then gestured with Alonzo's Peacemaker and her own revolver. Cimarron, followed by both women, began to make his way down the sharply sloping rimrock toward the mouth of the canyon and the three men holed up near it.

"Hey, look!" Dusty Atkins shouted from behind a deadfall where he had taken cover. "It's Julia and Rhoda, and by God, they've got the deputy."

Tolliver rose from behind a pile of rocks near the canyon's entrance. "Howdy, Julia, Rhoda. I sure never did expect to see either of you ladies out here, and certainly not in each other's company, given the fact that though my brother courted you, Julia, he went to Rhoda from time to time for recreation. How come?"

"I decided to come after Murdoch myself," Julia declared. "I had some trouble with this deputy here and realized I needed help. So I went to see Rhoda and she agreed to help me run Murdoch down, since she too wanted to get even with him for causing Al's death.

"We had just arrived here—drawn to the spot, I might add, by the sound of all the shooting—and we found this lawman lying up there on the rimrock all tuckered from his climb up out of the canyon. Now, boys, Rhoda and I are willing to turn him over to you in exchange for Murdoch."

Cimarron caught the eager glint in Tolliver's eyes and saw the sour smile form on Dusty Atkins' face.

"With all due respect, Julia," Obadiah Hoyt said slowly, "me and the boys here have first claim on Murdoch. We were the ones who caught up with him, and now that we've got him trapped in there like a treed coon—"

"A bird in the hand's worth two in the bush," Rhoda pointed out.

"Depends on what kind of bird it is," Obadiah argued. "Now that bird named Murdoch, he's a real valuable bird to every last one of us for our own particular reasons. But this lawdog—he's not much more than a nuisance, and if we can just keep him under wraps and out of our hair, we can all concentrate on what is, and damn well ought to be, our main goal: killing Murdoch."

Julia was about to say something when the thunder of pounding hooves ripped through the air. Murdoch, mounted on his buckskin, came galloping out of the canyon's mouth, the gun in his hand blazing into deadly life.

"Shoot him," Obadiah cried in evident alarm. He fired but missed Murdoch.

"He's getting away," Rhoda screamed frantically as she also fired at Murdoch and also missed her target.

As the still-shooting and still-galloping Murdoch was swallowed up in the thick cloud of dust being raised by his buckskin, Dusty Atkins shouted, "After him!"

The three men began to run toward their horses.

"Come on, Rhoda," Julia cried, and started around the slope. "Let's get our horses."

"What about him?" Rhoda pointed with her guns at Cimarron.

"To hell with him! It's Murdoch we want. Let's ride."

As both women ran from him, Cimarron started for

the canyon, intending to retrieve his black. He halted abruptly when Atkins, aboard his dun, drew rein, cursed the two women and Murdoch all in one angry breath, and took steady aim at him.

Cimarron raised his hands.

8

Atkins cursed Cimarron, claiming he was preventing him from riding down and killing Murdoch.

"One of the others will get to kill the son of a bitch," he muttered morosely as he kept his gun trained on Cimarron. "And I'm the one who wants him the worst."

"I'm not so sure you're altogether right about that, Atkins," Cimarron said as he continued to stand with his hands held high in the air. "Your friend Tolliver, it seems to me, has a damned good reason to want to get even with Murdoch. It was his brother who was hanged, thanks to Murdoch. And Al Tolliver was old Obadiah Hoyt's nephew, so the old man's also got good reason to want to murder Murdoch. Then there's the fair sex to consider. Julia Sinclair told me that she and Tolliver were fixing to get married, and Rhoda Ford, as I understand it, used to warm Tolliver's bed from time to time. They've no love for Murdoch either. You're just one of the pack, Atkins. You may find yourself having to stand in line to kill Murdoch."

Atkins muttered another curse under his breath. "Al and me were close as sardines in a can. We'd rode some long trails together, and some pretty tough ones too. When you share the hard times along with the good with another fellow—well, living like that builds a strong bond between men."

As Atkins continued reminiscing about his friendship

with Al Tolliver, Cimarron's thoughts raced to think of a way to get out from under Atkins' gun. Without moving his head, he surveyed the now-empty area.

". . . if only Al hadn't shot that teller to death while we were robbing that bank back in Arkansas, he'd most likely be alive right this very minute." Atkins was saying. "It's not the least bit likely that there'd be a price on his head—nor on mine neither—but for that killing. Banks are robbed just about every day and people seldom offer any reward for the robbers. But once killing's involved . . ."

If I could somehow spook that dun Atkins is aboard, Cimarron thought, maybe I could get his gun away from him before he has a chance to settle his horse down.

". . . and that's all Al ever meant to Murdoch—money. The cash he'd get for bringing Al in. But Al meant a whole lot more than that to me, I can tell you." Atkins dismounted and stood facing Cimarron. "Good friends are hard to come by in this old world," he observed. "And Al was the best friend I ever had. I would have trusted him with my life and he would have trusted me with his. That's how close the two of us were. So I don't care how good a reason anybody else thinks they've got to gun down Murdoch to pay him back for what he did to Al—I figure I've got the best one, which, put plain, is to avenge the death of a tried and true friend of mine."

Atkins said no more. He merely gestured to Cimarron that he was to back up and sit down in front of a tree. When Cimarron had done so, Atkins took up a position some distance away and proceeded to divide his attention between his prisoner and the distant horizon, toward which the others had headed when they rode out after Murdoch.

Some time later, when Atkins set about building himself a cigarette, Cimarron thought he saw his chance. He was ready to make his move as Atkins was about to light his cigarette. But he was only halfway to his feet when Atkins, despite his preoccupation with his cigarette, pack of brown papers, and pouch of tobacco, dropped all three and fired, deliberately aiming high so that his round smashed into the tree trunk a foot above Cimarron's head.

"Try that again and you're a dead man," Atkins told him in a cold quiet voice. "Maybe," he continued speculatively, "I ought to just shoot you now and have done with it."

Cimarron, who had resumed his sitting position as a result of Atkins' warning shot, tensed.

"But maybe Tolliver and his Uncle Obadiah have something else in mind for you. If they do, they'd be fretful to find I'd already gone and killed you." Atkins bent down and retrieved the cigarette he had built and the makings. He pocketed the latter, and his eyes never leaving Cimarron and the gun in his hand never moving, he thumbed a wooden match into bright red life with his free left hand and lit his cigarette.

He was smoking his fourth cigarette that afternoon when Cimarron caught sight of the riders approaching.

Murdoch's pack horse, which had apparently been retrieved from the cottonwoods, was being led by one of the riders, but there was no sign of Murdoch. Another horse was being led by one of the other riders, and when the group had come closer to him, Cimarron was able to make out the body that was draped over that horse's saddle. Having recognized the other riders as Bill Tolliver, Julia Sinclair, and Rhoda Ford, he knew who it was who was not returning under his own power: Obadiah Hoyt.

"Did you get him?" Atkins shouted to the others as they approached him, their faces solemn, none of them speaking.

"He got away from us," Bill Tolliver answered as he drew rein and got out of the saddle. "But before he did, he killed Uncle Obadiah."

Atkins swore.

"Which makes one more score I've got to settle with him," Tolliver stated, his expression grim.

"How could he get away from you?" Atkins raged, his frustration showing in the tense tone of his voice. "There were four of you and only one of him. He couldn't have gotten away from you!"

"Nevertheless, he did," Julia said as she dismounted.

"He slipped through our fingers as slick as smoke," Rhoda said as she got out of the saddle. "We almost had him and then he rode around a bend and by the time we rounded the same bend—*poof*! He was gone."

"Will you give me a hand with the burying, Dusty?" Bill Tolliver asked. "I'll have to lay Uncle Obadiah to rest out here instead of taking him back to the farm, because I'm not about to stop chasing Murdoch, not now I'm not."

"Uncle Obadiah wouldn't want you—us—to give up," Julia stated, and then watched with Rhoda and Cimarron as Tolliver removed his uncle's body from the horse and placed it over his shoulder.

"You ladies," Dusty said, "keep your guns on this lawdog. Shoot him if he so much as sweats."

Then, as Dusty and Tolliver made their way toward a towering cypress growing in the distance, Cimarron started to lower his hands.

"Keep them up!" Rhoda snarled at him, and he immediately raised them again.

"You heard what Dusty said," Julia reminded him. "You make one false move and both of us will fill you full of lead."

Cimarron *tsk-tsked*. "Ladies, I'm surprised at the pair of you. You should both be at home tending to your knitting instead of running around out here in this Godforsaken country toting guns that might go off and hurt somebody bad."

"Is that what happened to you?" Rhoda asked him, pointing with her free hand to the scar that marred the left side of Cimarron's face. "A stray bullet left you looking like that, did it?"

"Nope. Nothing half so exciting as that caused this scar. My pa gave it to me."

"Your pa?" Julia echoed, a startled expression on her

face. "What sort of father would do a thing like that to his son?"

"Oh, it was all an innocent-enough accident," Cimarron explained. "What happened was we were, Pa and me, branding a crop of calves one time down on the home place. Me, I was just a boy and I had caught a calf that was scared out of its wits. I was sitting on him and trying hard to hold him down when he up and threw me like a feather in a big wind. He got clean away from me. Pa got mad and said some not-so-nice words, and then he swung the red-hot iron he had in his hand. He wasn't looking where he was swinging it and it raked my face, and this here scar's the legacy left me by a man who had him a real wildcat of a temper he never could control."

"By the time Bill's through with you," Julia ventured, "you might have more than just that one scar."

Cimarron's gaze flicked back and forth between the two women. "What might that mean?"

"Bill was real upset about us losing Murdoch's trail," Rhoda replied. "On the way back here he had an idea."

"A good idea," Julia amended.

"He said you probably knew where Murdoch was headed after he left Wetumka," Rhoda continued. "He said in case we didn't catch up with Murdoch in Wetumka, you could tell us where he planned to go after he left there."

"I don't know anything about Murdoch's plans other than he's on the way to Wetumka."

"Bill thinks you might know why Murdoch was going there," Julia ventured. "And what he planned to do once he got there."

"Bill said you'd tell us what you knew, or else," Rhoda added.

"Or else?" Cimarron prompted.

"Or else," Julia said, "he'd find a way to make you tell us what we need to know. A way, I gather, that might leave you with, as I said before, more than that single scar on your face."

"But it doesn't have to come to that," Rhoda said

quickly. "I mean, you can just tell us what we want to know and that way you won't get hurt."

"Bill's not a mean man, Cimarron," Julia declared. "It's just that he's determined to get Murdoch, and he'll do whatever becomes necessary to accomplish that goal—including torturing information out of you if you force him to do that."

"There's not a thing about Murdoch I can tell him," Cimarron said, "other than that he paid me to ride with him as far as Wetumka."

"I don't believe you," Julia snapped.

"Neither do I," Rhoda said. "And neither will Bill."

Cimarron was about to protest once again that he knew nothing about Murdoch's plans, but before he could do so, Julia said, "Somebody's coming."

"It's that kid who was at the road ranch," Rhoda declared.

Cimarron glanced over his shoulder and saw Alonzo Hicks aboard his mule, Pegasus, approaching. Cradled in Alonzo's thin arms was his dog, Prince.

" 'Afternoon, Miss Ford," Alonzo said shyly as he rode up to Cimarron and the women. " 'Afternoon, ma'am," he said as shyly to Julia and then to Cimarron, "Howdy."

Prince yelped as Alonzo shifted position on his mule. Cimarron's keen eye noted the way the dog's left front leg dangled awkwardly.

"What happened to him?" he asked Alonzo.

"Pegasus kicked him," Alonzo answered. "His leg's busted. But I don't mind carrying him till it mends. He's not so heavy as he looks."

"Oh, the poor little thing," Julia exclaimed, and reached out to pet Prince.

The dog snapped at her.

"Stop that," Alonzo ordered the animal. "The lady's just trying to show you some pity." To Julia, "I'm sorry for the way he treated you, ma'am. It's not that he's naturally ornery. It's just that he hurts bad and his hurtin' makes him mean."

"Child, you should shoot that animal," Rhoda advised. "It's plain to see that the poor thing's in misery."

"I couldn't do that, Miss Ford," Alonzo said. "Prince and me—we're pals. Besides, even if I wanted to shoot him, I couldn't because you've got my gun that Cimarron took off me back along the trail aways."

"Oh, I didn't know this gun was yours." Rhoda handed Alonzo his Peacemaker, keeping her own revolver.

"Ladies," Cimarron began, "if you two will just give me half a chance I can maybe fix the kid's mutt for him. But I can't do it while my hands are reaching for the clouds."

Rhoda and Julia exchanged glances, and then Rhoda told Cimarron to go ahead and do what he could for Alonzo's dog.

"But watch yourself," Julia admonished him. "You try anything and we'll shoot."

"To kill," Rhoda added bluntly.

Cimarron lowered his hands, went over to Alonzo, and gingerly took the dog from his arms. Prince snarled deep in his throat and snapped at Cimarron as he examined the animal's leg.

"Get down, boy," he ordered Alonzo. When Alonzo had done so, he handed the dog back to him. "Now what I want you to do ... Put that damned Peacemaker down." When Alonzo had put the gun down on the ground, Cimarron continued, "Sit down and hold him tight. I'll be right back."

When he returned, Cimarron was carrying two short, slender pieces of wood he had broken from the branch of a sycamore. He untied his bandanna and ripped it into two pieces; then, as Alonzo held Prince and the dog struggled to free itself, snarling and snapping all the time, Cimarron deftly set the dog's leg. After placing the splints on both sides of the animal's leg, he tied them in place with the two pieces of his bandanna.

"Let go of him," he ordered Alonzo.

The boy released Prince, picked up his Peacemaker, and stood up. "Look at that," he cried, a broad smile on his face. "Why, he's walking around almost as good as before Pegasus busted his leg."

Cimarron watched the dog hobble about on its splinted leg. Then, thinking of the bowie knife in his boot, he glanced at Julia and Rhoda. They were watching with delight as Prince, carefully shepherded by a solicitous Alonzo, continued to hobble about and nip occasionally at his splinted leg.

Slowly, Cimarron bent over and surreptitiously reached for the knife in his boot. But he straightened with a sheepish grin as both Julia and Rhoda suddenly turned toward him and he found himself once again staring into the muzzles of their guns. He raised his hands.

He was still standing with his hands in the air, Alonzo was sitting with Prince, who lay panting on the ground, and Julia and Rhoda were discussing the intricacies of fancy needlework when Atkins and Tolliver returned nearly an hour later.

"Who's the kid?" Atkins asked.

"His name is Alonzo Hicks," Rhoda answered. "He was at Scovill's road ranch when I got there. He and Murdoch were hitting it off pretty well, as I recall."

Cimarron laughed, a short harsh sound.

"What's funny, lawman?" Atkins asked him.

"Murdoch and the kid may have been getting along real well at the ranch," Cimarron replied, "but later—well, later was another story. The kid tried to kill Murdoch. I stopped him from doing so—took his gun away from him. And then Rhoda took his gun from me along with my own when she got the drop on me."

"Why'd you do it?" Tolliver asked Alonzo. "Try to kill Murdoch, I mean. You've got it in for him for some reason the same as the rest of us have?"

"I was after his money," Alonzo said. "I've not got much of my own and I expect I've got a long way to go before I finally settle down."

"Let me tell you something, kid," Tolliver said, shaking a stiff finger in Alonzo's face. "You leave Murdoch alone, you hear? The four of us here, we're after him, and for more good reasons than just money, and we don't want any competition from you."

"Just steer clear of us," Atkins warned. "Or you'll find yourself in a peck of trouble."

Alonzo said nothing.

Tolliver turned his attention to Cimarron. "Where was Murdoch planning to go after he left Wetumka?"

"I just got through telling the ladies here," Cimarron said wearily, "that I don't know anything at all about where Murdoch was going after he got to Wetumka. I can only tell you boys the selfsame thing."

"He's lying," Atkins snarled.

"What was Murdoch planning to do once he got to Wetumka?" Tolliver asked, ignoring Atkins' remark.

"I've not the least idea," Cimarron answered.

"He knows," Atkins said. "The pair of them were partners. Murdoch would have told him."

"He didn't," Cimarron insisted.

"We'll find out whether or not he did," Atkins muttered ominously. "Me and Bill here talked it over after we planted his Uncle Obadiah, and I came up with an idea about how to make you talk if it turned out you were reluctant to." Atkins turned to the women. "Keep him in your gunsights. I'll be back presently."

Cimarron, keenly aware of the two guns in the women's hands which were aimed at his midsection, watched Atkins go to his horse and open his saddlebag. He saw him take a horseshoe, a pair of pliers, and a length of rope from it and then saunter back.

"It's time to tie him up now," Atkins announced; then, after dropping the horseshoe and pliers on the ground, he and Tolliver proceeded to tie Cimarron to a locust tree.

Minutes later, Atkins had a fire going. As Cimarron, his back pressed against the tree's trunk and his hands tied tightly behind it, watched, he gripped the horseshoe with his pliers and held its two ends in the flames.

Cimarron felt sweat begin to ooze from under his arms. He knew what Atkins was going to do. He's going to use that horseshoe of his, when it's hot enough, as a branding iron, he thought. The muscles in his shoulders and neck began to stiffen in anticipation of the pain he expected to experience soon. He remembered the awful agony he had felt that day that was lost now in the dead past when his father's branding iron had raked his face, searing his flesh and permanently scarring his face. It had happened in one single angry instant, but the pain had remained with him for days. This time, he suspected, it would be worse because it would not all be over in an instant.

Atkins rose, pointing the orange-white ends of the horseshoe at Cimarron. "Open his shirt, Bill."

Tolliver stepped up to Cimarron and ripped open his shirt, baring his chest. He stepped back, giving way to Atkins, who appeared in front of Cimarron, a faint smile on his face.

"Where's Murdoch headed after Wetumka?" he asked in a low tone. "And what's he planning on doing once he gets to Wetumka?"

"I told you before and I'm telling you now," Cimarron said, his eyes on the glowing ends of the horseshoe, only inches away from his chest. "I don't know."

Fear stiffened his body as Atkins moved the makeshift branding iron closer to his chest. But then his fear was supplanted by a rising tide of fury—an onrushing and overwhelming wave of hatred for Atkins, his self-appointed torturer.

Both his fear and his fury dissolved then under the onslaught of searing pain that roared through him as Atkins brought the ends of the horseshoe into contact with his chest. He gasped, fighting hard to suppress the scream that was trying to erupt from his throat as his flesh sizzled and his nostrils filled with the pungent stench of burned flesh and hair.

"Tell him what he wants to know, Cimarron," Rhoda pleaded as a shudder of revulsion ran through her body.

"Then he'll let you go," Julia said. "What is Murdoch to you, Cimarron? You needn't try to protect him from us."

"Save yourself," Rhoda demanded. "Give us Murdoch."

Cimarron heard the horror both women were obviously feeling lurking behind their pleas. "You'll have to keep on cooking me, I reckon," he muttered between clenched teeth, "on account of I don't know the answers to the questions y'all keep on asking me."

"I'll heat this up and try again," Atkins said, holding up the horseshoe, which still glowed but far more faintly now.

As he started back to the fire, Alonzo spoke up. "I can tell you folks what you have a hankering to know."

All eyes turned to Alonzo.

"What do you know about Murdoch?" Tolliver asked Alonzo.

"You stop tormenting him"—he indicated Cimarron—"and I'll tell you. I didn't want to say nothing, seeing as how I was after Murdoch myself, but . . ." Alonzo swallowed hard and continued, "Back at the road ranch before Miss Ford got there, Mr. Murdoch, he told me . . . Will you promise not to hurt Cimarron anymore?"

Atkins glanced at Tolliver, who nodded almost imperceptibly.

"Go ahead, kid, talk," Atkins growled.

"Mr. Murdoch, he's headed south to Texas after he leaves Wetumka."

"What was he going to Wetumka for in the first place?" Tolliver asked.

"He wanted to see his—his wife before he traveled on to Texas," Alonzo answered.

"Now that we know what we need to know," Tolliver said, "we can move out after Murdoch."

"What about Cimarron?" Rhoda asked tremulously, her eyes fixed on the blackened spot on his chest that had been burned by Atkins' fiery horseshoe.

"We'll leave him here," Atkins replied. "We've no need of him now. Or we could kill him." He gave Tolliver a glance.

Tolliver shook his head. "I don't want his blood on my hands. Murdoch's will be enough to last me a lifetime." He beckoned to Alonzo. "You're coming with us, kid."

"I'd just as soon ride alone," Alonzo declared hesitantly with a sidelong glance at Cimarron.

"After Murdoch, you mean," Tolliver said. "Well, we can't have that. We don't want a pint-sized would-be robber doing us out of the revenge we're all out after."

"You can ride beside me," Julia told Alonzo. "We'll keep each other company. Won't that be fun?"

Cimarron, when the others had ridden away, strained at the ropes that bound him to the locust tree, but found he couldn't free his hands. Undaunted, he continued trying to fold first one hand and then the other into as small a space as possible in the hope that he could slip one of them through the rope. After nearly ten relentless minutes of trying, he gave up. He simply leaned against the tree, looking up at the sky, which had begun to fill once again with snow blossoms, and listening to the silence, broken only by the faint whine of the rising wind as it blew across the empty land.

His head swiveled as far as it could go in both directions as he searched the landscape for sign of any other person in the area who might be of help to him. But he saw no one. He resumed his efforts to free himself, cursing the recalcitrant rope that wouldn't give even a fraction of an inch, and longing for—almost lusting after—his bowie knife, which was lodged in his right boot. Since there was absolutely no way he could reach it, his knife might just as well have been somewhere on the other side of the world.

No way?

He remained motionless for a moment, thinking. Was there really no way that he could get his hands—or a hand—on his knife? He looked down at his dusty boots. A grim smile slowly formed on his face. He bent his knees and began to ease his body down toward the ground. His hands scraped against the tree as he performed the maneuver, and the muscles in his arms began to ache. He found it was slow going because there was almost no slack in the rope. The skin was being scraped from his hands by the rough bark of the tree, and the pain that resulted was a minor version of the major pain that still throbbed in the center of his chest where his flesh had been so badly burned. His knees continued to bend little by little until finally he was kneeling on the ground. He thrust his buttocks back against the tree; then, with his upper torso leaning forward as far as the rope would permit, he slowly eased his legs backward until they were straddling the tree trunk.

He felt exultation ripple through him as he succeeded in working his bound hands down toward his boots. By shifting his body to one side, he was able to place his groping fingers on the top of his right boot. Then, by slow and painstaking maneuvering, he managed to slip the fingers of his right hand into his boot. As they closed on the hilt of his knife, he rested for a moment, not moving a muscle, almost able to taste the freedom he was seeking.

He began to withdraw the knife from his boot, straining against the rope and the tree as he did so. Drops of sweat blossomed on his face and fell to the ground as he continued his efforts. Finally the knife slid out of his boot. He shook it free of its sheath, and then, manipulating it with great care, he managed to place its sharp blade against the rope around his wrists. Using only one hand, he began to saw at the rope, simultaneously moving the rope back and forth as far as he could by stretching and then withdrawing his other hand.

He worked doggedly all afternoon, while the sky filled with clouds that turned from white to gray to black. He hoped to free himself before the impending snow began to fall. But he failed to meet his self-imposed deadline. Fat flakes of snow were falling when he finally succeeded in severing the rope that bound him to the tree. As it gave way, he fell forward. When he hit the ground, pain flamed in both his burned chest and raw wrists, and he stifled an anguished cry. He lay on the ground for a moment, not moving, hardly breathing, thinking, I did it. I'm free.

And then he gingerly rose to a sitting position. He drew the ends of his ripped shirt around his chest, then buttoned his buckskin jacket over them. He sheathed his knife and returned it to his boot. Shakily, he got to his feet and stood there, leaning with one hand pressed against the tree trunk for support. He turned his face to the sky and let the cold snow, which was falling more thickly now, refresh him. He drew a deep breath and then went wavering unsteadily toward the mouth of the canyon. Inside, he went up to his black and put his hand on the stock of his Winchester, which rested in his saddle boot. At least I've got this gun left, he thought as he leaned heavily against his horse; his .44 was now in Julia Sinclair's hands.

Then, after boarding the black, he turned and walked it out of the box canyon, thinking of Murdoch—thinking too of the additional hundred dollars Murdoch had promised to pay him when they reached Wetumka. There's only one way I'm going to get my hands on that other hundred, he told himself, and that's if I can catch up with Murdoch wherever he is and ride the rest of the way with him to Wetumka. But even if I manage to do that, he thought, frowning, maybe Murdoch won't want to pay me the other hundred. He's liable to claim I don't deserve it, since he got part way to where he was going on his own with no help from me. He shrugged. If I don't make a try at earning that money, I'll never see it. If I do make a try for it, it just might wind up in my pocket.

He put heels to the black and the horse went loping through the thickening snow, heading west.

9

Cimarron hadn't gone far when he thought he saw something in the swirling snow. He peered through narrowed eyes and was just able to make out the dark figure in the white world up ahead of him. His hand went to his Winchester.

He turned his black to the right and rode in among some trees, where he drew his rifle from its boot and sat his saddle, waiting. When his black blew, he leaned down and clamped his left hand around its nose to silence it.

Squinting, he stared into the snow. A moment later the figure he had glimpsed materialized not far away. He gazed in surprise at Alonzo Hicks, who, aboard Pegasus and trailed by the hobbling Prince, was riding slowly in an easterly direction.

He moved the black out and went loping through the snow toward the boy. Alonzo, at the sound of his approach, drew his Peacemaker and aimed it unsteadily in his direction. But when Cimarron called his name, the boy broke into a smile and thrust his gun back into his waistband.

"What are you doing here?" Cimarron asked as he drew rein beside the boy.

"I got away from them." Alonzo answered without bothering to explain who "them" were. "I was on my way back to where they left you tied up."

"Why were you?"

"I was going to turn you loose," Alonzo replied, looking embarrassed.

"Well, now," Cimarron drawled, "that comes as a surprise."

"Well, it oughtn't to. You did me a favor when I was in need and I figured it was only right to turn around and do one for you in turn."

"The favor I did you—you mean splinting your pup's leg?"

Alonzo nodded.

"You did one other thing for me, as I recall. Those lies you told about Murdoch heading down to Texas after he visited his wife in Wetumka—those sure were two of the tallest tales I ever heard told. They were lies, weren't they?"

Alonzo nodded and looked down at the ground. He kicked at a stone he found lying at his feet. "What they were doing to you—I tried to think of a way to make them stop hurting you. Those stories about Mr. Murdoch were all I could come up with."

"Well, they worked just fine."

Alonzo looked up. "How'd you get loose all by yourself?"

Cimarron told him.

Alonzo whistled through his teeth in apparent admiration. "I'd never have been able to do a thing like that. Not in a whole month of Sundays, I wouldn't."

"I'm obliged to you, boy, for thinking of me in my time of trouble. There's not many folks around these days like yourself who'll put themselves out for a stranger in trouble."

"Like I said, I figured I owed you."

"You don't anymore. We're even now." Cimarron gave Alonzo an appraising glance. "What are you fixing to do now that you've found me and I'm not in need of your help?"

Alonzo pursed his lips, was thoughtful for a moment; then, "I guess I'll just keep on westering." A pause. "What did you have it in mind to do?"

"I'm going to try to catch up with Murdoch, if I can find him, and then mosey on with him to Wetumka as we were doing before we ran into that trouble on the trail back there."

"I don't suppose you could use some company, could you?"

"I reckon company wouldn't hurt me none. I take it you're talking about riding along with me?" When Alonzo gave a hesitant nod, Cimarron asked him if he knew where Tolliver, Atkins, and the two women were.

"They're due west of here. Why?"

"Well, I have no hankering to run into that bunch again. Four against one's not odds to my liking. Last time I went up against them I did real poorly, as you saw. We'll ride to the south and bypass them. Only there's one thing we ought to get straight before we set out."

"What might that be?"

"I want you to promise me you won't try any more funny business if and when we happen upon Murdoch. Is that understood?"

Alonzo hesitated briefly and then nodded. "I promise."

"Good," Cimarron said with relief, failing to notice that Alonzo had the first two fingers of both hands crossed.

As they rode out, the boy remarked, "There's another fellow with Miss Ford and the others."

"There is?"

"He said his name was Dawson. He came galloping up to us like he was in an awful hurry to get somewhere. But he stopped to talk. It was when all those folks were talking together that I slipped away and started back to where they'd left you all tied up."

"That bunch can't be too far ahead of us."

"They're not."

Cimarron and Alonzo had covered less than another mile when Cimarron saw the dull-orange glow of a campfire in the distance that was streaked with sometimes thin and sometimes thick waves of white.

"That's them," Alonzo declared. "They said they were

going to make camp for the night on account of the storm."

"Let's us head down that other way so as to steer clear of those folks," Cimarron suggested.

They rode due south for a time and, a little later on, changed direction and headed southwest. But their progress was slowed by the increasing intensity of the storm, which was sending snow flying across the land on the rough wings of a savagely whipping wind.

Cimarron turned up the collar of his buckskin jacket and pulled his hat down low on his forehead as his black plowed on through the drifts. Alonzo, behind him, rode with his body bent and his arms wrapped tightly around the neck of his mule, which occasionally brayed its dismay into the dark night surrounding them.

Cimarron pressed on, glancing over his shoulder from time to time but barely able to make out the figure of Alonzo astride Pegasus. He stopped once, dismounted, and used his bare hands to melt the ice crystals that were forming on his black's eyelashes; then he did the same for Alonzo's mule. When both animals were able to see clearly again, he chose not to board his black. Instead, he gripped the animal's reins and began to lead it through the night, walking directly in front of the animal to shield it, as both of them moved directly into the wind that had begun to howl around them.

He traveled that way for some time and then looked back. The black blocked his view. He stepped to one side, sinking almost to his knees in a deep drift, and then, able to see only Pegasus but no sign of Alonzo, he called the boy's name. Receiving no answer, he shouted Alonzo's name into the night, only to have it borne quickly away on the ripping wind.

He left his black ground-hitched and made his way back past the mule, which stood with its head drooping. He saw no sign of Alonzo and no tracks at all, because the wind was sending the snow swirling across the surface of the land. He walked on over the ground he had just covered, and then began to walk in a circle that grew wider as he continued searching.

He found Alonzo almost by accident, nearly falling over the boy. He was huddled at the thick base of a shin oak with his arms wrapped around Prince. The dog's head emerged from the protective covering for a brief moment before it disappeared again from sight.

"Get up," Cimarron ordered as he reached down and pulled Alonzo to his feet. "What the hell are you doing way back here?" he asked, aware that his anger was born of the fear he had been feeling concerning Alonzo's possible fate.

"Prince," Alonzo managed to get out between noisily chattering teeth. "He couldn't get through the drifts. I went back for him."

"You could have died," Cimarron bellowed over the noise of the punishing wind. "And all for a damned mongrel dog."

"He's all I got," Alonzo cried, tears beginning to ooze from his eyes. "Pegasus and Prince, they're the only family I got now. I couldn't leave him out here to die."

Cimarron picked up both the boy and dog. "I reckon you couldn't," he said, not sure if the wind had whirled his words away before the boy had heard him. Carrying Alonzo and the blanketed Prince, he started back to his black and Pegasus. He had not gone far, his head lowered against the sting of the sleet that was mixing now with the snow, when Alonzo yelled, "Look!"

He looked but saw nothing.

"Over there!"

Cimarron, looking in the direction Alonzo was pointing, was finally able to make out the outline of some kind of building. He turned sharply and started toward it. As he came closer, he was able to see that it was a windowless log cabin, long abandoned, judging by its state of severe disrepair. Reaching it, he pulled open its sagging door, which was hanging by its rotting leather hinges, and entered the building.

He lowered Alonzo, who still held Prince in his arms, to the floor and took a wooden match from the cuff of his jeans. He thumbed it into life and discovered that the dirt-floored cabin contained a few pieces of handmade wooden furniture, a rope bed, a half-empty woodbox by the hearth, and a barrel that was half full of apples. "Light a fire," he ordered Alonzo, and handed the boy two matches. As Alonzo set to work building a fire in the hearth, Cimarron went outside and led his black and Alonzo's mule around behind the cabin. He tethered them out of the wind to a lone tree that grew behind the cabin. After returning to the cabin, he shut the door against the storm and wedged it in place with the blade of his bowie knife.

"We'll wait out the storm in here," he told Alonzo, who was hungrily devouring an apple he had taken from the barrel.

Later, when Alonzo was asleep on the rope bed Cimarron had insisted he take and Cimarron was almost asleep on the floor near the fire, his hat and rifle beside him, the door was shoved open. A heavyset man wearing a cartridge belt containing a Smith & Wesson blued and ribbed-barreled .44 army revolver came lumbering into the cabin, swirling snow like a white halo around him.

Cimarron seized his rifle and sprang to his feet. "Don't move, mister!"

The man raised his hands.

"Cimarron?" the awakening Alonzo whispered.

Cimarron ordered the boy to get up and shut the door, which Alonzo obediently and promptly did, using Cimarron's bowie knife as a door stop.

"Who am I up against?" the intruder asked in an uneasy voice.

Cimarron identified himself and Alonzo. "Who are you?"

"My name's Duke Dawson. I don't mean anybody any harm. I was out there in the storm and I spotted this place and decided to take shelter in it. I didn't know it was already occupied. If I'm not welcome, I'll be on my way. Only don't shoot me."

"Cimarron, he's the man I told you about," Alonzo said. "Mr. Dawson was at the camp when I ran off."

Cimarron recalled Alonzo's reference to the man who

had earlier galloped into the camp of Tolliver and the others.

"I thought you looked familiar, boy," Dawson declared. "But at first I wasn't sure you were the same young 'un that ran like a rabbit from that camp back along the trail." He peered thoughtfully at Cimarron. "And you're Cimarron." Dawson scratched his stubbled chin and moved closer to the fire, turning his back to it and raising the canvas coat he wore so the flames could warm him. "They had one or two choice things to say about you, Cimarron."

"Who did?"

"The folks back at that camp I mentioned, the camp this kid ran off from. Fellows named Tolliver and Atkins and two women named Sinclair and Ford. They were free talkers, all four of them were. They told me they were trailing a man named Sam Murdoch and they also told me why they were. They said you were a thorn in their side, but they'd put you out of their way." Dawson gave a hearty laugh. "They're in for a big surprise if and when they find out you got loose from that tree they tied you to. You going after them? You planning to get even with them for what they did to you?"

"Nope."

"We're going to Wetumka," Alonzo volunteered, "to hunt for Mr. Murdoch."

"Boy, you'd do well to learn how to keep your private business to yourself," Cimarron said gruffly.

"I was just—"

"Don't chastise the boy for being friendly," Dawson admonished Cimarron. He unbuttoned his coat and turned to face the fire.

"Did Tolliver and the others say they'd seen sign of Murdoch?" Cimarron asked.

Dawson shook his head.

"What's that mean?" Cimarron persisted. "They didn't see Murdoch's sign or they didn't say whether they had?"

"They said they'd seen no sign of him. Which is no wonder. The snow's covered every track left by man or

146

beast. Once it stops, though, then a fellow will be able to track real easy." Dawson turned around. "Well, I reckon it's time I was on my way again."

"You're welcome to bed down here for the night," Cimarron said. "There's room enough."

"That's neighborly of you, Cimarron, but I think I'd best be moving on."

"It's a real bad night out there. One that's hard on both men and beasts."

Dawson buttoned his coat. "I don't mind a bit of weather. Neither does my dapple. So I'll be pushing on. I only came in here for a brief respite from the storm and to chase the chill from my bones." Dawson settled his hat on his head, hitched up his gunbelt, and as Alonzo removed Cimarron's knife and opened the door, went outside into the still falling snow.

"That man must be loco to head out into this storm of his own free will," Cimarron mused as Alonzo secured the door. "Or else he's got pressing business somewhere up the line."

"I'm sure glad I don't have to be out in all that snow," Alonzo remarked as he returned to the rope bed. "I'm bushed."

As he lay down on the floor in front of the fire again with his rifle beside him, Cimarron realized that the boy wasn't the only one who was bushed. Almost instantly he slipped into a dreamless sleep that quickly and totally blotted out the world around him.

When Cimarron awoke, he found himself staring into a dead fire. Shivering, he got up and opened the cabin door to find bright sunlight streaming down on the drifted snow outside. Almost blinded by the reflection of the afternoon sun on the snow, he blinked and took a step backward.

"Wake up, boy," he said. "Storm's over. It's time to move out." He went into the cabin and picked up his hat and rifle from the floor. Only then did he notice that the rope bed was empty. The kid's an early riser, was his first thought as he clapped his hat on his head.

He's lit a shuck, was his second disquieting thought. He hurriedly left the cabin and made his way around it—to find no sign of his black or of Alonzo's mule.

He scanned the ground but the soft surface of the snow was unbroken and unmarked. Which means, he thought grimly, the kid snuck out sometime during the night before it stopped snowing. He ran off my black, looks like. Which means he don't want me to be able to trail him. Which in turn means one thing for sure: he's on his way to Wetumka. And there's only one good reason why he is. And the name of that reason is Murdoch. He means to relieve the man of his money just like he tried to do once already. He swore and, carrying his Winchester, set out in search of his horse.

Don't much matter which way I go, he thought as he made his way through the deep snow that sucked at his boots and slowed his progress. There's just no telling which way that horse went when he was run off. But he hadn't gone far when he spotted the black, which looked like a huge ebony blot on the snow that covered a distant hillside. He plowed on, the horse watching him warily as it stood more than hock-deep in the snow.

When he reached the animal, he patted its neck, booted his rifle, and began to lead the black back to the cabin. "One good thing about all this snow," he told the horse, "is it kept you from traveling very far. The Lord alone knows what I'd've done if you'd up and disappeared altogether on me."

Once back at the cabin, he went inside and came out a few minutes later with his hands full of apples. He fed these to the horse, who almost ate his hand along with the fruit, a testament to the degree of its hunger. When the horse was finally satisfied, Cimarron went back inside and gathered up more apples, eating them as he rode west.

He wondered as he rode how much of a head start Alonzo had on him. Could be hours, he thought. Maybe less. He pulled his hat down low on his forehead to shield his eyes from the blinding glare of the sun on the snow's smooth surface. The black beneath him blew as it plowed gamely on, its hot breath condensing into two clouds of steam in the frosty air.

At dawn the following day, Cimarron forded Wewoka Creek. The sun was rising when he rode into Wetumka and headed straight for the local livery. As he rode past sleepy merchants busily shoveling snow from the boardwalk in front of their shops, he had the main street to himself, since drivers of wheeled vehicles were apparently unwilling to tackle the snow-clogged thoroughfare.

"Your horse is looking pretty poorly," the leather-aproned farrier greeted him as he entered the livery, dismounted, and drew his rifle from its boot. "His legs are cut up pretty bad."

"The snow had melted in a few places I passed, but then it froze over again. It was the crust of ice on top of the snow that cut him up like that. You got some kind of soothing balm you can put on him to help him heal?"

"I'll take as good care of him, mister, as I would were he mine. Of course, the doctoring will cost you extra on top of his board and feed."

"I'll pay your price, providing it's fair."

The farrier quoted a price and Cimarron agreed to it.

As he was about to leave the stable, a horse in one of the stalls at the rear of the building nickered and he glanced in that direction. "That dapple back there," he said to the farrier. "When did it get here?"

"In the middle of the night. Just after midnight it was."

Cimarron described Duke Dawson to the farrier. "Was that what the man looked like who was riding him?"

"That's the man. Is he a friend of yours?"

"Nope. I just happened to run into him back along the trail, and though I never did see his horse, he mentioned it was a dapple. Be seeing you."

"When will you be back for your horse?"

"Can't say for certain. But I can say I will be back.

Till I do, you grain him, water him, and rub him down real good."

Outside on the street again with his rifle in his hand, Cimarron looked around and then started down the snowy boardwalk. He went inside the first restaurant he came to and sat at a table against a wall from which he could see both the front door and the entrance to the kitchen at the rear of the room. He leaned his rifle against the wall, and when a young woman wearing a spotless apron and a pert white cap appeared beside him, he ordered a steak, boiled potatoes, bread, butter, and coffee. He was just finishing his meal when he looked up to see Sam Murdoch striding into the restaurant.

"Howdy," Cimarron said as Murdoch spotted him and froze. "I see you made it to Wetumka all on your own and in one piece."

"No thanks to you," Murdoch snarled, and turned to go.

"Come over here, Murdoch," Cimarron ordered. "I want to have a talk with you."

Murdoch turned, his hand reaching for the doorknob.

"Murdoch."

The man looked over his shoulder.

Cimarron beckoned, and as Murdoch joined him at his table, he said, "Have a steak. They do them good here. I just ate one."

But when the waitress appeared from the kitchen, Murdoch turned to her and ordered, "Coffee."

"What's the matter, Murdoch? You're not hungry?"

"Seeing you again has spoiled my appetite."

"Now, is that a nice thing to say to a man who was—and still is—ready, willing, and able to lay his life on the line for you?"

"A helluva lot of good you did me. I could have been killed six times before Sunday and you'd still be busy climbing up out of box canyons and dallying with outlaw ladies."

"That was all a matter of bad timing and worse luck, and you damned well know it was, Murdoch. Now, what I had in mind to talk to you about if I ever ran into you again, it was this. I'm still interested in earning that other hundred dollars you promised to pay me for bodyguarding you. I've no other means of support at the moment because, like I told you, I quit my job as a deputy marshal for Judge Parker's court."

"I have no further need of your services, Cimarron."

"You may be wrong about that, Murdoch. Tolliver and Atkins and the two women with them are still trailing you though the snow's slowed them down some. And another thing—"

As Cimarron suddenly sprang to his feet, Murdoch spun around to find himself facing Alonzo Hicks, who stood grim-faced and stiff-legged in the doorway of the restaurant. The gun in the boy's hand never wavered as he squeezed the trigger and lead and fire spurted from the weapon's black muzzle.

An instant before Alonzo fired, Cimarron had kicked over the table at which he and Murdoch had been sitting. As the dishes on it struck the wooden floor and smashed, the table knocked Murdoch down. Alonzo's shot missed its mark and buried itself harmlessly in the wall.

Alonzo cocked his revolver and prepared to fire again at Murdoch, who was scrambling rapidly on hands and knees along the floor in an attempt to take cover. Cimarron picked up and hurled a chair, which struck Alonzo's arm, knocking the six-gun from the boy's hand. At that moment, the waitress appeared in the kitchen doorway, let out a scream when she saw what was happening, and fled out the front door.

Cimarron sprinted around the fallen table, heading for Alonzo, who was down on his hands and knees and reaching for his weapon under a table. Cimarron first seized the boy's gun, which he placed in his holster, and then picked Alonzo up by the scruff of his neck and dragged him to his feet. Alonzo tried to fight him, his limbs flailing helplessly as Cimarron held him out at arm's length and off the floor.

"He's getting away," Alonzo cried, pointing a shaking finger.

Cimarron glanced over his shoulder and saw Murdoch scurrying toward the kitchen door. "Murdoch," he yelled. "Hold it right there!"

When Murdoch continued his headlong flight, Cimarron, still holding tightly to Alonzo, grabbed his rifle and pulled its trigger, intending to fire a warning shot above the fleeing Murdoch's head. But his gun didn't fire. Cimarron pulled the trigger a second time and again the gun didn't fire. Throwing Alonzo over his shoulder, Cimarron went racing into the kitchen after the vanished Murdoch. He collided with a heavy wooden table and both he and the table went down. Falling, he made a grab for Alonzo, who had escaped from him and was scampering toward the back door. A moment later, he got his feet under him, regained his balance, retrieved his rifle, and went chasing after the boy. He caught him an instant before Alonzo reached the back door. "I ought to brain you, boy," he snarled, and then slammed Alonzo up against the wall. "Don't you move," he warned his captive.

He examined his Winchester, puzzled by the weapon's failure to fire. Finding no apparent fault with the gun, he ejected a shell and examined it. "Well, I'll be damned," he exclaimed when he discovered to his amazement that all the powder had been removed from behind the slug. Now, who the hell, he wondered . . . He looked up at Alonzo.

The boy shrank back against the wall.

"Last night," Cimarron said. "Before you ran off. You did this to my gun."

Alonzo blanched but said nothing.

Cimarron grabbed a fistful of the boy's jacket and shook him. "Didn't you?"

Alonzo nodded.

Cimarron fought hard against the fury that was rising within him, wanting and not wanting to hit the boy. "You could have got me killed."

Alonzo remained silent.

"Why, boy? Why'd you do it?" Cimarron asked as he reloaded his Winchester, first making sure that the cartridges in his belt hadn't been tampered with.

To Cimarron's surprise, Alonzo's features contorted and he began to cry. Tears filled his eyes and spilled over to run down his cheeks. He wiped them away but they kept coming. His small body shook with sobs.

"Speak your piece, boy."

"I wanted to make sure you couldn't stop me."

"Stop you from what—from killing Murdoch? That's what it looked like to me you were bent on doing just now. Not just robbing the man like you said you meant to do the first time you went for him, but killing him." A thought suddenly occurred to Cimarron. "That first time you shot at Murdoch—you weren't trying to rob him like you said you were, were you? You meant to kill him, didn't you?" When Alonzo said nothing, "Answer me, boy."

"Yes! I did mean to kill him—both times. It wasn't his money I was after that first time like I said it was. It was his life I wanted."

Alonzo struggled to stifle his sobs but failed to do so. "Murdoch killed my pa," he got out in a storm of sniffles and sobs.

"Your pa?" More puzzled than ever, Cimarron could only stare at Alonzo, whose weeping had ceased as suddenly as it had begun.

"Al Tolliver."

"Al Tolliver," Cimarron heard himself echo foolishly without the faintest degree of understanding.

"Al Tolliver was my pa."

"Wait a minute. How could Al Tolliver be your pa when your name's not Tolliver but Hicks?"

"I'm a bastard."

"You're a—" Cimarron almost collapsed in laughter as he thought that he really couldn't argue with the label Alonzo had given himself. And then it dawned on him that the boy had used the term in the literal, old-fashioned sense of the word.

"Al Tolliver was my pa," Alonzo repeated glumly. "I

never knew my ma. She turned me over to Mr. and Mrs. Hicks right after I was born, and they brought me up like I was their own. Only just before Pa—I mean Mr. Hicks, my foster father—died not long ago, he told me what my real mother had told him a long time ago. Mr. Hicks told me that Al Tolliver was my real pa and that he lived on a farm in Arkansas near his Uncle Obadiah Hoyt. Mr. Hicks said it was only right for me to know the truth now that I was about to be left alone. Mr. Hicks told me where to go to find my real pa and tell him I was his son so that maybe Mr. Tolliver would look after me, at least till I got my growth.

"Well, I went. But when I got where I was going, Mr. Hoyt, he told me that he was real sorry but that my pa had been riding the owlhoot trail and a man named Sam Murdoch had caught him to collect the bounty on his head and that my pa had been hanged." Tears flooded Alonzo's eyes again. He began to tremble and then to shudder.

"So I found out I had nobody, thanks to Mr. Murdoch," he wailed, covering his face with his hands. And then he took his hands away and stared up at Cimarron. "I made up my mind to go after Mr. Murdoch for what he did to my real pa. I was in Fort Smith when I found out he'd been there and was on his way to Wetumka. So I started trailing him."

Alonzo sniffed and continued, "I never did get a chance to know my real pa and he never got a chance to know me. Oh, I know maybe he wouldn't have wanted to have any truck with me. If he had he probably would have come around to look me up a long time ago. But from what I heard I'm not his only bastard. His Uncle Obadiah told me my pa was always a caution where the girls were concerned." Alonzo almost smiled. "He said my pa was his most favorite nephew even though he'd daddied enough kids to start a school by the time he was twenty years old. It sure is going to please me to be able to tell my pa's Uncle Obadiah about how I gunned Mr. Murdoch down."

Cimarron thumbed his hat back on his head. "You're never going to get that pleasure, boy."

"Oh, I'll get Mr. Murdoch. Sooner or later, I will."

"What I meant was Obadiah Hoyt's dead." Cimarron explained that Murdoch had killed Hoyt.

"Then I've got even more reason than before to kill Mr. Murdoch. For my pa and for his Uncle Obadiah too." Alonzo suddenly made a dash for the door.

"Oh, no, you don't," Cimarron yelled, and scooped Alonzo up, throwing him over his shoulder. He marched out of the restaurant to where the boy's mule was tethered to a hitch rail and his dog, Prince, stood shivering in the snow.

"Let go of me," Alonzo shouted, pounding his small fists against Cimarron's broad back.

Prince, startled by the boy's shouting, began to bark and to snap at Cimarron's boots.

"Sic him, Prince!" Alonzo shouted. Then, as the snarling dog snapped again at Cimarron's boots and Cimarron hop-skipped away from the animal, "Where are you taking me to?"

"To right here," Cimarron answered as he set Alonzo on his feet. He pointed to the sign nailed above the entrance to the one-story building directly in front of him. It read: JAIL.

Alonzo tried to make a run for it.

But Cimarron caught him by the collar and marched him into the building.

10

The Creek Indian warming his hands in front of a Sibley stove looked up as Cimarron ushered Alonzo into the jail.

"Howdy, Roley."

"Howdy yourself, Cimarron. What have you got there?"

"This here's a fellow name of Alonzo Hicks, and I'd like for you to lock him up and hold him awhile for me."

"He doesn't look like a troublemaker," Roley declared, eyeing Alonzo. "And besides, I don't have jurisdiction over him since he's white. This slapdash jail the town pays me too damn little to man has never before played host to anybody who was white. White people—they're your concern, Cimarron. I might get in trouble with Marshal Upham back in Fort Smith if he learned I locked up somebody white."

"You won't get in any trouble, Roley," Cimarron assured the Creek jailer. "You won't on account of you're acting under my authority in this matter. If there's any blame to be taken, I'll do the taking—but I promise you there won't be any. Now, will you do like I said and lock him up in that storeroom over there that serves you as a cell?"

"Well, I guess—hope—you know what you're doing,

Cimarron," Roley remarked somewhat doubtfully. He gestured. "Step inside that storeroom, son."

Alonzo reluctantly did as he was told. Then, just as the storeroom door was about to shut, he glared at Cimarron and asked, "What about my dog?"

Roley gave Cimarron a puzzled glance. "What about his dog?"

Cimarron went outside, and when he returned, he was carrying Prince by the scruff of his neck. He handed the dog to Alonzo, then stepped aside so that Roley could close and lock the storeroom door.

"What about my mule?" Alonzo asked, cradling Prince in his arms.

"What about his mule, Cimarron?" Roley asked.

"I'll see to him," Cimarron promised Alonzo.

Roley shut and locked the storeroom door. "Do you mind telling me what's going on, Cimarron?"

"It's kind of a long story, Roley, and I've not got time to tell it all to you. But I'll tell you this much: I'm on the trail of a bounty-hunter you might have heard tell of. His name's Sam Murdoch."

"Sure, I know Murdoch. As a matter of fact, I ran into him a little while ago. He was on his way over to the restaurant. We had a talk. I told him I had a bunch of fresh dodgers in my office and I told him he was welcome to drop in and take a look at them. But he said he wasn't interested. Which kind of surprised me since, like you said, Murdoch's in the business of bounty-hunting.

"So I asked him if he had retired and taken to living off the fat of the land, and he up and answered me that he had indeed. I've no idea what he meant by that, but he was grinning from ear to ear when he said it just like a cat lapping cream."

"I ran into Murdoch over in the restaurant a little bit ago, but he gave me the slip. I was planning on seeing if he's staying at the hotel here in town."

"He is. He told me he rented a room when he hit town last night. But you'd better hurry."

"Why?"

"Murdoch said he was planning on leaving town today, right after he'd had himself something to eat. Fact is, he seemed mighty itchy to me. Now, Murdoch always struck me as the kind of fellow who could take life any old way it came at him, but this time when we met he seemed to me to be as restless as the tip of a cat's tail. Since you say you've been trailing him, I reckon I can understand now why he seemed to be getting ready to pitch a fit."

"It's not just me that's trailing him. There are a few others too. Matter of fact, that tad you've got locked up in there happens to be one of them."

"How long am I supposed to hold on to him?"

"Till I get back to claim him. Which shouldn't be too long, if I have any luck and can find Murdoch fast."

Cimarron left the jail. After turning Alonzo's mule over to the farrier at the livery, he went to the mercantile to purchase a box of cartridges for Alonzo's Peacemaker. On his way to Wetumka's only hotel, a two-story clapboard structure with an elaborate false front, Cimarron filled the empty chambers of the gun's cylinder and then returned it to his holster.

He spoke to the desk clerk in the lobby. The clerk, his uneasy eyes on the rifle in Cimarron's hand, told him that, yes, a Mr. Sam Murdoch was registered and he had been given room number two on the first floor.

His rifle in his hand, Cimarron made his way across the lobby and up the stairs. At the door of room number two, he was about to knock when he heard the sound of voices coming from inside the room. He listened, able to make out a few words here and there.

". . . and I've finally caught up with you."

He recognized the voice as that of Duke Dawson, who had briefly visited the cabin he had shared with Alonzo the night before.

"How did you—"

Cimarron didn't understand the rest of the words, but he recognized the voice as Murdoch's. *Now what the hell has Dawson got to do with Murdoch?* he wondered.

"It was easy. I checked downstairs. You shouldn't have registered under your own name, Murdoch."

"I'll split the take with you."

"It's too late for that now. Now I want it all and if I don't get it, you're a dead man, Murdoch."

"Put down that gun—"

Cimarron almost smiled, thinking that he had come just in time—just in time to earn the other hundred dollars that Murdoch had earlier offered him as payment for his protection. His right index finger closed on the trigger of his Winchester as his left hand closed on the knob of the door behind which Murdoch and Dawson argued. Slowly, he turned the knob and was gratified to find that the door was unlocked.

He drew a deep breath and then kicked the door wide open. He lunged into the room, his rifle rising, its barrel aimed at an obviously startled Duke Dawson. Dawson's revolver was aimed at Murdoch's head, and Murdoch stood stiffly in front of him with his hands raised. "Drop it," he ordered, and Dawson, after a brief moment of hesitation, did.

As Dawson's gun clattered on the wooden floor and Murdoch lowered his arms, Cimarron ordered Dawson to back up. When the man had done so, Cimarron moved forward, picked up Dawson's dropped weapon, and thrust it into his waistband. "Which one of you wants to tell me just what the hell's going on here?" he barked.

He was answered by silence on the part of both men.

"This is none of your affair, Cimarron," Murdoch told him.

"It's not? I say it is, since you hired me to try to save your hide from manhunters like Dawson here. Which is what I just did. So I'm laying claim to that other hundred dollars you promised to pay me."

"You want the hundred?" Murdoch's hand plunged into his pocket. When it emerged, he counted out a hundred dollars from the wad it held and offered the money to Cimarron. "You got it."

Cimarron took the money and pocketed it.

"Now we can call it quits," Murdoch said, watching Cimarron with wary eyes.

"Nope, we can't, Murdoch. Not yet. Not till the matter here at hand's settled and my curiosity's satisfied." He gave Dawson an inquiring glance. "Talk, mister."

"I knew I had trouble on my hands when I ran into you at the cabin during the snowstorm," Dawson muttered. "Tolliver and the others told me about you, but they all thought you were still tied up to the tree back by that box canyon where they'd left you to rot. Then, after I left them and came upon the cabin—there you were, dammit. I'd planned on spending the night in that cabin when I spotted it, but I knew I'd better keep moving when that kid you had with you said you both were on your way to Wetumka after Murdoch."

"Why did you throw down on him?" Cimarron asked, indicating Murdoch.

"Why?" Dawson gave a guttural laugh that contained no merriment. "I threw down on him because he did me wrong."

"Cimarron, you've got the other hundred dollars I promised to pay you," Murdoch interjected. "Take it and get the hell out of here."

Cimarron ignored Murdoch. "What do you mean?" he asked Dawson. "How did Murdoch here do you wrong?"

"I ran into him some time back in Sasakwa in Seminole Nation. We got to talking. One thing led to another and the next thing the two of us knew was that we'd decided to rob the stage that was leaving Sasakwa that same day. We did. We trailed it out of town and then we stopped it and robbed the passengers. We—"

"This is between the two of us, Dawson," Murdoch practically shouted.

"Not anymore it's not. Now we've got this lawdog to deal with." Turning his attention to Cimarron, Dawson continued, "We were lucky that day. One of the passengers on the stage was a diamond merchant who turned out to be carrying a big bunch of uncut stones, which we relieved him of. The man had a fortune in gems on him. Murdoch and me had earlier agreed to split the take fifty-fifty, but right after we sent the stage on its way, Murdoch gave me the slip and I've been hunting him ever since either to get the diamonds from him or to kill him for doublecrossing me."

Before Dawson could say anything more, Cimarron spoke to Murdoch. "You told me some time back, as I recollect, that it was just south of Sasakwa in Seminole Nation that you caught Al Tolliver and lost Dusty Atkins."

"I did. That was right after I ditched Dawson. I'd been trailing the two of them when I met Dawson in Sasakwa."

"What happened to the diamonds?" Cimarron asked.

Murdoch gave him a crafty look. "There is no point in lying to you—not at this unfortunate juncture. I have the diamonds on me." He patted his pocket. "I buried them just outside of town, figuring I'd come back for them when things settled down. I dug them up this morning."

"You have them," Dawson exclaimed gleefully. "Let's see them."

Murdoch pulled a leather pouch from his pocket. He opened its drawstring and poured the diamonds it contained into the palm of his other hand and then held them out for Dawson and Cimarron to see.

"I have a proposition to make to you two," he said evenly. "We'll divide up the diamonds among us and then go our separate ways."

Dawson was about to say something but apparently thought better of it. He remained silent, his speculative eyes on Cimarron.

Cimarron held out his hand to Murdoch.

Murdoch smiled and proceeded to divide the diamonds into three equal piles on his palm. He picked up a third of them and was about to place them in Cimarron's outstretched hand when Cimarron shook his head and said, "Put them all back in their pouch and then hand me the pouch."

"What?" Murdoch stared at him in disbelief.

161

"I want all those diamonds," Cimarron told him.

Murdoch slowly replaced the diamonds in the pouch. As slowly, he drew its drawstring and then held it out to Cimarron.

As Cimarron reached for it, Murdoch suddenly drew his revolver, which had been hanging holstered on his hip, and aimed it directly at Cimarron's gut.

"Throw that rifle on the bed," he ordered Cimarron. "Throw Dawson's gun and the one in your holster alongside it."

When Cimarron had placed the three guns on the bed, Murdoch warily made his way around him and then opened the door. "If either of you two try to rush me once I leave this room, I'll blow your brains out. That's a promise. One I'll keep." He slipped out into the hall and slammed the door behind him.

Cimarron and Dawson exchanged glances as they heard a key turn in the lock. Then Cimarron picked up the guns, holstering the Peacemaker he had taken from Alonzo and returning Dawson's gun to his waistband. With his rifle held at the level of his hip, he fired a single blast, which blew a hole in the door, smashing the knob and lock fixture.

"Let's go get those diamonds, Dawson," he yelled, and went through the door, which was swinging back and forth on its hinges.

Dawson raced after Cimarron, demanding the return of the gun Cimarron had taken from him earlier. But Cimarron, as he bounded down the steps to the main floor, ignored Dawson as well as the spluttering desk clerk at the foot of the stairs, who wanted to know who had done the shooting and why.

Once outside, Cimarron spotted Murdoch racing down the snowy street and into the livery. He ran after the man. Dawson followed him, still fruitlessly demanding the return of his gun. When they reached the jail, Cimarron turned sharply, his rifle trained now on Dawson, and barked, "Inside!"

Dawson opened his mouth to speak but said nothing when Cimarron rammed the barrel of his Winchester into the man's chest. As he marched Dawson into the jail, Roley, the startled jailer, almost knocked over his Sibley stove.

"Open the storeroom," Cimarron said. He shoved Dawson into the room, slammed the door, and ordered Roley to lock it, which the Indian promptly did. "I'll be back for him and the kid," he told the Creek.

"Who the hell was that one?" Roley yelled as Cimarron sprinted for the door. "What's he went and done?"

Cimarron never answered the man's questions. Instead, he ran outside and veered sharply in the direction of the livery. Before he had gone more than a few steps, he halted at the unwelcome sight of the four riders who were loping down the street toward him. It was too late, he knew, to hide. Julia Sinclair was pointing at him, Rhoda Ford's eyes and mouth were wide open in surprise as she stared at him, and Dusty Atkins and Bill Tolliver both had drawn their guns and aimed them directly at him.

He threw himself to the ground, rolled over, and came up crouching on one knee behind a wooden water trough. He had no sooner done so than a bullet from Atkins' gun slammed into the far side of the trough and water began to spurt through the hole made by the bullet. Cimarron held his fire as Julia and Rhoda dismounted and scurried, one after the other, into a dry-goods store directly across the street. Atkins fired again, but as he did so, his mount wheeled and his shot went wild. Cimarron, with his rifle's barrel propped on top of the trough, tracked Tolliver, who sprang from his saddle and took refuge in a narrow alley between the dry-goods store and a tin shop. Atkins struck his still-circling horse's head with his fisted left hand and then, raking the animal's flanks with his spurs, rode into the alley after Tolliver.

Cimarron's eyes shifted from the alley to the livery, which was a little bit farther up the street. He shifted position and looked at a lawyer's office directly behind him. He scrambled toward it, crouching, and burst into the building. "Where's the back door?" he demanded.

A nervous man as pale as ice pointed wordlessly to a curtained alcove, which Cimarron followed through to the back door and into an expanse of empty snow-covered land stretching all the way to the distant horizon.

He ran to the right, passing one building after another, until he reached the end of the row. He made his way to the right again, and when he reached the street, he peered around the edge of the building at the end of the row—and saw no one. He dashed across the street and then turned to the right again behind the row of buildings on that side of the street and went loping along behind them, hoping to find Murdoch still in the livery.

Before Cimarron reached the livery, Atkins rode out of the rear of the alley where he and Tolliver had taken refuge. When Atkins spotted Cimarron, he took aim. Still running, Cimarron fired a snap shot from his rifle at Atkins' horse. The round slammed into the animal's skull, sending red blood and white bone flying through the air and spoiling Atkins' aim. As the horse went down, Atkins lost his gun and was nearly buried beneath the bulk of the animal, which was thrashing wildly about in its death throes.

Cimarron ran up to the stunned Atkins, picked up his gun from where it lay in the snow, and threw it away. Then, as Atkins staggered groggily to his feet, Cimarron swung his rifle. Its barrel caught Atkins squarely on the side of the head, downing the man. Leaving Atkins where he lay unconscious on the ground, Cimarron back-trailed to the livery. Gripping his rifle by its barrel, he used its stock to smash a window, through which he quickly climbed into the building.

He made his way past stalls and a cold forge, heading for the front of the building, searching as he went for Murdoch. When he reached an empty stall, he suddenly halted and stared at the farrier with whom he had spoken earlier and who was now crouching inside the stall, a look of terror on his contorted face.

"Don't shoot," the man cried, holding up both hands as his wide eyes pleaded soundlessly with Cimarron.

"I'm hunting a man," Cimarron told him, and described Murdoch. "He here?"

"Oh, Lord a'mighty," moaned the farrier. "I never have done nothing bad enough to deserve this. Mister, why don't you just go away and leave me be?"

Cimarron stepped inside the stall and placed the muzzle of his Winchester against the cowering farrier's throat. "Answer my question."

The farrier pointed to a tall pile of bulging burlap bags stacked directly opposite the empty stall. Then, in a hoarse whisper, "He was saddling his horse when the shooting started out front. He took a look out the door and then he ducked back inside here and hid himself behind those sacks of grain."

Cimarron turned and left the stall. Taking up a position behind one of the stout wood posts that supported the loft, he barked, "Come on out of there, Murdoch!"

For a moment, there was no response. Then a gun thundered, and the round Murdoch had fired from his place of concealment buried itself in the post in front of Cimarron.

"Drop it!"

Cimarron froze. His head swiveled to the left and he saw Bill Tolliver standing in the open doorway of the livery with his gun in his hand. Cimarron dropped his rifle.

"Get rid of those other guns too," Tolliver ordered him.

Cimarron had removed Dawson's revolver from his waistband and was reaching for Alonzo's Peacemaker which was in his holster when another shot sounded. Cimarron realized that this one had come from the opposite direction and had been directed at Murdoch. He turned his head and saw Atkins framed in the broken window at the rear of the building. As he stared at the man, Atkins grinned and was about to fire his gun, which he had evidently retrieved, at Murdoch who was plainly visible to him from where he stood. But before he could fire a second time, Murdoch fired first, and Atkins flew backward, disappearing from the window, his gun falling inside the livery.

Cimarron threw himself to one side, hit the pile of grain sacks hard, and toppled them down upon Murdoch. Even before they had all fallen, he had retrieved his rifle and dropped down behind some of the sacks next to Murdoch. "Throw it down," he ordered. When Murdoch had dropped his gun, Cimarron sent it skittering across the floor with the muzzle of his rifle.

"Julia!" yelled Bill Tolliver, who still stood to one side of the livery's doorway. "Rhoda!"

"He's rounding up more guns," Cimarron muttered to Murdoch. "If you know what's good for you, you'll stay right where you are till the shooting stops and I tell you you can come out into the light of day again. You got that?"

Murdoch nodded.

Cimarron picked up a sack of grain. Using it as a shield, he rose and made a rapid zigzag run toward the open door of the livery. Halfway to it, Julia appeared in the doorway and fired his own .44 at him and missed; then Rhoda also appeared and fired at him, but her round rammed into the sack of grain he was holding tearing it but doing him no harm.

Cimarron ran faster, grain beginning to spill from the sack in his hands like air from a punctured balloon. He hurled the sack of grain and it struck the three people in the doorway, toppling all of them, as well as causing Tolliver's gun to go off and Rhoda's to fall to the ground.

He halted in the doorway, breathing hard, and stared down at Tolliver and the two women; they were all staring back up at him. He kicked the revolver from Tolliver's hand, and as Rhoda made a lunge for her fallen gun, he kicked it out of her reach. "Stand up," he ordered the trio as he relieved Julia of his .44 and holstered it.

They stood.

"Back up!"

They backed up.

"Come on out of there, Murdoch," Cimarron yelled over his shoulder.

When he got no response, he glanced over his shoulder and swore when he saw Murdoch scurry out from behind the toppled grain sacks, retrieve his gun, and go racing toward the broken window at the rear of the livery.

"Inside!" he ordered his three prisoners. He swiftly herded them into the livery, picked up Alonzo's Peacemaker he had been forced to drop earlier, and tossed it to the farrier, who was still crouched in the empty stall. "Guard them good," Cimarron ordered the man. "If they get away from you, it's your ass that'll suffer the consequences." Without waiting for a response from the thoroughly startled farrier, he ran to the rear of the livery and quickly climbed out the window through which Murdoch had disappeared only a moment earlier.

He halted and held his fire. Atkins, lying on the ground and bleeding badly from a chest wound, had seized the escaping Murdoch's left ankle with both hands and held on to it.

Murdoch bellowed in rage and swung his gun. As the bounty hunter's iron smashed into his skull, Atkins screamed and let go. But before Murdoch could resume his run, Cimarron stepped up to him and slammed the barrel of his Winchester into the man's ribs.

Murdoch stiffened and dropped his gun. His hands rose in the air.

Cimarron looked down at Atkins. The man's eyes were closed. His head was bloody and broken. He hunkered down, keeping his rifle on Murdoch, and placed two fingers of his left hand against Atkins' neck. He felt a faint pulse.

Atkins' eyes eased open. They blinked, focused. "Cimarron."

Cimarron said nothing.

"I'm finished," Atkins murmured, the words a sigh.

Still Cimarron said nothing.

"Tell you something," Atkins whispered, his eyes clouding. "Now that I'm dying—it's time I told the truth. It wasn't Tolliver."

"What are you talking about?" Cimarron asked him.

"Al Tolliver," Atkins answered. He gagged and then spit blood. "Al Tolliver didn't kill that bank teller during the robbery. It was me did it."

Cimarron and Murdoch exchanged glances.

"I never let on that I did it," Atkins said weakly. "If I had and Murdoch had ever caught me, I'd've hanged."

"You let your best friend hang," Cimarron accused, "for something you did."

Atkins squeezed his eyes shut, groaned, and then nodded almost imperceptibly.

Cimarron turned toward the window and yelled to the farrier to bring his three prisoners around behind the livery. When Tolliver, Rhoda, and Julia stood nearby, he said, "Atkins has a story to tell that you three ought to hear. Tell them what you just told me, Atkins."

When Atkins had done so, Tolliver gave a strangled cry and fell on the dying man. As he began to beat him, Cimarron reached down, seized Tolliver by the coat collar, and hauled him to his feet. As he shoved Tolliver away, Rhoda lunged at him. Before he could thrust her aside, she had his .44 out of his holster.

She fired once and then dropped Cimarron's gun.

Cimarron picked it up and returned it to his holster. "He was already dead," he told Rhoda. "You didn't kill him."

Rhoda collapsed in tears, her face covering her hands. "He killed Al," she sobbed. "Just as if he'd put the noose around Al's neck with his own two hands."

"How could he do that?" a stunned Julia asked of no one in particular. "How could he let Al go to the gallows for a murder he didn't commit?"

Tolliver stood staring down in disgust at the dead Atkins. "Why didn't Al say something? Tell the truth about who really killed that bank teller?"

It was Cimarron who answered Tolliver. "Your brother and Atkins were friends. Him keeping quiet about the killing, it says something fine about your brother. It says he gave up his own life for his friend. I don't know many men who'd go and do a thing like that."

"How does Atkins' confession make you feel, bounty hunter?" Rhoda snapped, wiping the tears from her eyes with two small fists.

"Don't blame me for what happened," Murdoch growled. "Blame the law. Blame the judge and jury."

"Let's go," Cimarron said, taking Alonzo's Peacemaker from the farrier. "Be seeing you," he told the man as he marched Murdoch and the others to the jail. There he asked Roley, the jailer, to let Alonzo and Duke Dawson out of the storeroom. When the pair stood before him, he told Alonzo, who was holding Prince in his arms, what had just happened and about the confession Atkins had made.

"So your pa wasn't a murderer, boy, whatever else he might have been."

Tolliver repeated, "His pa? What are you talking about, Cimarron?"

"Your brother, Al, was this boy's pa," Cimarron stated, and gave Tolliver a brief description of Alonzo's background. Turning to Alonzo, he said, "You're free to go, boy. Here's your gun." He returned Alonzo's Peacemaker. "Do you have any idea where you'll go now that this shindig is over and done with?"

Alonzo shook his head. "I got no place of my own now. I told you that. All I've got is this here broken-legged dog and a mean old mule. But I'll find me someplace one of these days."

"You've already found yourself an uncle," Tolliver said quietly, "meaning me, of course."

"You could have been the son that Al Tolliver and I might have had," Julia declared in a low voice, her eyes on Alonzo. "If Al had lived and if—if things had been different." She paused a moment; then, "You could come home with me, Alonzo, until you make up your mind about what to do and where to go. I'd like that. It would be almost like having your father with me once more. You see, Alonzo, your father and I were very much in love."

Cimarron said, "You'd be doing the lady and yourself a kindness, boy, were you to take her up on her offer."

Alonzo hesitated, but then, as Tolliver gave him a nod and a smile, the boy told Julia, "I reckon I'll ride along with you. With you and Uncle Bill." He glanced shyly at Cimarron and said, "I'm sorry for having been such a bother to you."

"We all are," Tolliver said, not quite able to meet Cimarron's steady gaze. "It wasn't that we wanted to hurt you. We wanted—"

"We wanted revenge against Murdoch," Julia interrupted. "I hope you can find it in your heart to forgive us all, Cimarron."

"I've got me enough burdens to carry about in this old world without adding grudges and bygones to my pack," he told her. "What's done is done—forgotten too, as far as I'm concerned."

"Then it's time we started for home," Julia declared, putting one arm around Alonzo's shoulders and the other around Bill Tolliver's waist.

Rhoda drew Cimarron aside. She gripped his arm and, standing on the tips of her toes, kissed him on the cheek. "Thanks for what you did for me."

"I didn't do anything for you, honey."

"Oh, yes you did. You could be taking me in on a charge of murder. You and I both know Dusty Atkins was still alive when I shot and killed him."

"I don't have the foggiest notion of what you're talking about, Rhoda honey."

"If that's the way you want it . . ." She kissed him again.

"They're all yours now," Cimarron said to Charley Burns, as he turned Murdoch and Dawson over to him several days later at the jail in the basement of the Fort Smith courthouse. "Them and these diamonds they both stole." Cimarron handed Murdoch's leather pouch containing the stolen gems to the jailer. "And here's the five dollars I owe you."

"I don't get it," Charley said, taking the money Cimarron handed him and pocketing it. "Last time we talked, you'd quit riding for Judge Parker. And now here you are just like always turning in prisoners you rounded up out in the Territory. I just don't get it."

"To tell you the truth, Charley, neither do I. Be seeing you." As Cimarron started to swing into his saddle, he heard a window being raised and looked up to see Marshal Upham framed in his office window. For a moment, the two men merely stared at each other and then Upham called out, "I'll be in your debt, Cimarron, if you'll take the time to come up here to my office."

As Upham closed his window, Cimarron hesitated for a moment and then, shaking his head, made his way into the courthouse and up the stairs to Upham's office.

As he entered, Upham waved him into a chair and sat down behind his desk. "I wasn't all that sure I'd ever see you again."

Cimarron said nothing.

"Who were those two men I saw you turn over to Charley?"

Cimarron identified Murdoch and Dawson and then gave Upham a brief history of what had happened since he had left Fort Smith.

"You told me you were through with being a lawman," Upham remarked when he had finished. "I'm glad to see that you're not."

"What makes you think I'm not?"

"Those two prisoners you brought in. They do."

"Oh, them. Well, after I'd settled their hash, there were some friends of mine—a fellow named Tolliver, two ladies named Julia and Rhoda, and a tad named Alonzo Hicks—who happened to be headed east, so I thought I'd ride along with them to keep them company. I figured I might as well bring in Murdoch and Dawson, since I was heading in this direction."

"I see." Upham thoughtfully stroked his chin. "Are you waiting for me to get down on my knees?"

"What say, Marshal?"

"You want me to beg you to agree to be a deputy again?"

"Now, why would I want you to do a thing like that? The job's not worth a hill of beans. It could get a fellow killed. It don't pay a decent wage, and the fact that it gets in the blood of a man like me—" Cimarron fell silent, damning himself for having said too much.

"A man like you is a decided and proven asset to this office and to Judge Parker's court," Upham stated solemnly. "I know that you and I have had our differences over the years, Cimarron. But I want you to know that I—and I know that I also speak for Judge Parker in this matter—value you highly. I *will* get down on my knees if that's what it will take to get you"— Upham opened a desk drawer, removed Cimarron's nickel star from it, and held it out to him—"to take this back."

Cimarron looked down at the deputy marshal's badge shining in Upham's palm and then up at Upham. He held out his hand and Upham handed him the star.

"What made you change your mind?" Upham asked him.

For a moment, Cimarron was silent. Then, beginning to grin, he said, "A couple of things, Marshal. You'd look fairly foolish down on your knees begging me to be a deputy again, for one. And for another, well, after what I just told you happened to me out in the Territory, you can probably tell that I'm not much good at doing anything else but starpacking. And for still another—though I hate like hell to have to say this— who else but you'd have me, Marshal?"

Cimarron's grin widened, matched by the one that was spreading across Marshal Upham's face.

SPECIAL PREVIEW

Here is the first chapter from

CIMARRON
AND THE HIRED GUNS

twenty-second in the action-packed
CIMARRON series from Signet

1

Cimarron hunkered down in front of the fire he had built and slowly turned the spit. On it was the skinned and gutted carcass of a mule-eared jackrabbit. Fat fell from it into the fire, where it sizzled and popped.

While the early-morning wind sloughed through the loblolly pines, a jay screamed its shrill objections to his presence in its preserve. Cimarron was aware of the coyote that prowled stealthily among the trees, its jaws slavering and its nose quivering in response to the tantalizing smell of roasting flesh. That critter must be mighty hungry, he thought, else he'd not be showing that foxy face of his in broad daylight, since his kind are night feeders. He reached down and picked up the jack's head, which lay by his boots. He threw it into the underbrush and watched the coyote pounce upon it, pick it up in its sharp teeth, and go racing away with it, the animal's tail a tan banner waving behind it.

Cimarron continued turning the spit and swallowing the saliva that kept flooding his mouth as the jack's carcass turned from a soft golden color to a crisp brown. He removed the spit

Excerpt From THE HIRED GUNS

from the fire and, unable to wait for the meat to cool, took a bite. He gave a grunt and quickly spat it out, but it had burned his lips and tongue. He forced himself to wait, as steam curled up from the spitted carcass and the coyote returned to sit boldly not far from the fire, its flickering eyes on the spitted meat.

Finally, goaded by his hunger, Cimarron again bit off a piece of meat, and this time he was able to chew and swallow it. He took another bite and then another, stripping the flesh from the bones with his teeth and relishing the hearty though slightly gamy taste of his meal. When he had finished, he tossed the bony remains of the carcass to his companion, the coyote. Then he rose, kicked out the fire, and went to where he had left his black to browse the first green growth of spring that had appeared on the branches of some wild huckleberry bushes.

He led the animal down to the bank of the nearby stream, which was a tributary of the Grand River, and let the animal drink. Then, after pulling the horse's head up so that it would not drink too much, he swung into the saddle and continued his journey through Creek Nation.

"Don't be mad at me," he said softly to the snorting black as they moved out. "If I'd've let you drink your fill back there, you'd be likely to give out on me before we get to wherever it is we're going." And where exactly, he asked himself as he walked the horse west, are we going? Damned if I know the answer to that question. I reckon we'll just keep roaming like a bug on a hot night till we get someplace worth stopping for a spell or we find us a miscreant in want of arresting.

Cimarron, as he rode on, sat tall in the saddle, every inch of his lean and tautly muscled body relaxed, but ready to respond to whatever he might suddenly and unexpectedly face. His shoulders were broad above a thick chest and narrow waist, around which was strapped his black leather cartridge belt. In his oiled hip hoster rested his Frontier Model .44 Colt, from which he had cut away the trigger guard. The oiled holster allowed him the fastest possible draw, and the missing metal allowed him quick and easy access to the gun's trigger.

His large and bony-fingered hands, the reins wrapped around them, rested lightly on his saddle horn as he rode. His long legs loosely straddled the barrel of his black, and his low-heeled army boots were comfortably planted in low-slung stirrups.

Cimarron's bright-green eyes roamed the countryside, noting

Excerpt From THE HIRED GUNS

everything, missing nothing. His ears, which lay flat against his head, heard even the faintest sound made in his vicinity. His straight black hair hid them and buried the nape of his neck and his frayed shirt collar. His forehead was broad beneath the brim of his hat. His cheeks were slightly sunken on either side of a narrow flared-nostriled nose. Above his square and jutting jaw his lips were thin, a faintly grim line like a gash across his face.

The scar that marred the left side of his face ran from just below his eye down along his cheek, to end just above the corner of his mouth. It caught the eyes of anyone who looked at him, causing speculation about how that ridge of livid lifeless flesh had come to be there. The scar seemed to mock the handsomeness that more than one woman had seen in his decidedly masculine mix of features, and it made more than one man wonder uneasily if Cimarron were not a man best left alone.

His clothes were far from new. There was a button missing from his blue bib shirt. The knees of his jeans had faded to a faint blue-white and looked as if they might part at any minute. His black leather vest was scraped and scarred in places, and the black stetson on his head was sweat-stained and weathered. The blue bandanna he wore tied around the strong column of his neck was grayed by trail dust.

But his well-cared-for six-gun gleamed, looking as new as any that might be found on a storekeeper's shelf, and so did the '73 Winchester in his saddle boot.

He looked up at the sky. The sun was rising, turning some cirrus clouds from white to russet. On all sides of him the land stretched out, lying flat and unmarked by any ridge or hummock, to meet the sky. He felt dwarfed by the immensity of the land and the limitlessness of the sky as he continued riding west, pursued by the sun. In the distance ahead of him a pair of blue grouse took wing, flew across the empty land for a few yards, and then dropped down and out of sight in a clump of pale-green corn lilies.

It was early afternoon of a day that had grown surprisingly hot when Cimarron came within sight of Tullahassee. When he reached the town, he found it full of people going about their business or simply strolling and enjoying the warmth of the spring sun. He drew rein in front of the general store, dismounted, wrapped his reins around a hitchrail, and went

Excerpt From THE HIRED GUNS

inside; the small brass bell above the front door tinkled to announce his entrance.

"Good morning," greeted the clerk, from behind a counter piled high with colorful bolts of cloth. "What can I do for you, sir?"

"You can sell me some forty-four–forty cartridges."

"Happy to oblige." The clerk went to a shelf and returned with a box of cartridges, which he placed on the counter in front of Cimarron. "I see through the window," he said, "that you've got a rifle in your saddle scabbard. Will you be needing ammunition for it also?"

"Nope. These shells fit both my Colt and that Winchester of mine out there. Which means I don't have to take the trouble to tote two kinds of shells around with me. How much am I in your debt?"

The clerk quoted a price and Cimarron paid it. Then, after filling the empty loops in his belt with cartridges, Cimarron left the store. He had just deposited the box of cartridges in his saddlebag and was about to swing into the saddle when he heard a male voice call his name. He turned and looked across the street to where a man was stepping down from the boardwalk and hurrying toward him.

"Good to see you again, Cimarron," the man exclaimed. He offered his hand, which Cimarron pointedly ignored. "It's been quite a while since we last met."

"Are you still making a living by telling folks what the law says they can and can't do, Butler?"

"Do I detect a disparaging note in your voice, Cimarron?" When Cimarron didn't answer, Butler said, "I know you don't have any great love for me as a result of my having gotten that client of mine free of Judge Parker's court. I'm talking, of course, about Rollo Hayes, the man you arrested on a charge of horse stealing."

"You got Hayes off on a technicality," Cimarron pointed out. "But the man was as guilty as sin, and you and me and he and Judge Parker all knew it."

"I only did my best in defending my client. But I don't want to talk about the past, Cimarron. It's the present I'm concerned with at the moment."

"Be seeing you, Butler." Cimarron was about to thrust a boot into a stirrup when Butler's hand landed on his arm. He stiffened, staring at the lawyer.

Excerpt From THE HIRED GUNS

"I need the help of a lawman such as yourself, Cimarron. I'm having a legal problem with a man who lives outside of town. A man named Lou Drake."

Cimarron shook Butler's hand from his arm.

"You're sworn to protect the people of Indian Territory against the likes of Lou Drake, Cimarron. The fact that there has been bad blood between you and me in the past makes no difference at all in a case like this. I'm calling on you now for help and you are bound, as an officer of the court that has jurisdiction here to give me the help I require."

"And if I don't give it to you? What'll you do? Tell tales about me to Marshal Upham? Or to Judge Parker?"

"Look, Cimarron. Can't we just let bygones be bygones? Wipe the slate clean and start fresh?"

Cimarron glanced down the street, seeing it as an escape route. He sighed. "What's your problem, Butler?"

The lawyer broke into a broad grin. "I knew you'd help me out of a bad spot, Cimarrron. I just knew it." His hand landed again on Cimarron's arm.

Cimarron looked down at it and then up at the man.

Butler's smile faltered, faded. He removed his hand from Cimarron's arm.

"I asked you what your problem was, Butler."

"It's with Lou Drake, and it's not just my problem. Actually, it's my client's problem. I represent Len Hoffstatter, who owns the general store you just came from. He holds a note Drake signed and now Drake has defaulted on that note."

"So what do you need a lawdog like me for? Why don't you and Hoffstatter just ride on out to Drake's place and demand the payment you say's due?"

"We tried doing that very thing just last week. Drake ran us off. He and his wife and two sons. They pulled guns on us. They threatened to shoot us. There was no way we could get that family of deadbeats to listen to reason. But if you were to go out there with us, I'm sure Drake could be made to understand that he's in the wrong."

"All right, let's go, Butler. I'd like to get this matter over and done with just as quick as I can so I can be on my way again."

"Fine. I'll take my buggy and we can pick up Len Hoffstatter at his house on our way out of town."

* * *

Excerpt From THE HIRED GUNS

Cimarron, Butler, and Hoffstatter were met by three men with shotguns, and a woman, unarmed but scowling, as they rode up to the Drake cabin.

"Put those guns away, Mr. Drake," Butler shouted. "We mean you no harm. We've just come to let you have a talk with the law in the person of this deputy United States marshal named Cimarron."

"Did all the talking I intend to do the last time you were here, Counselor," shouted back the oldest of the three armed men.

"That's Lou Drake," Butler told Cimarron, indicating the man who had just spoken. "That's his wife, Merrilee, standing next to him, and flanking them are Drake's two sons. That's Bobby on the right and Mike on the left."

Cimarron got out of the saddle and beckoned to Butler and Hoffstatter, who got down from Butler's buggy and followed him. When he reached Drake, he pulled his nickel badge from his pocket and displayed it to the four people facing him.

"What for did you have to go and fetch the law?" Drake snapped, his eyes darting between Butler and Hoffstatter. "I told you—"

"Suppose you tell me exactly what this here dispute is all about," Cimarron interrupted, addressing Drake.

"I already told you," Butler said in an exasperated tone. "Drake has fallen behind on his note, which Mr. Hoffstatter, my client, holds, and Mr. Hoffstatter has therefore engaged me to foreclose on Drake's livestock."

"Butler," Cimarron said, "I'd be mighty obliged to you if you'd just shut your mouth and let me hear for myself what Drake here has to say."

Drake glanced at his wife and then back at Cimarron. "I told Hoffstatter I'd pay. Soon as I could, that is. My credit's allus been good. Or it was with Deke Masters, who owned the general store before he cashed in his chips and Hoffstatter took over the place. So was my word good—with old Deke."

"What's this talk about foreclosing on your stock, Drake?" Cimarron inquired. "What's your livestock got to do with the note in question?"

Drake gave Butler a fiery glare and answered, "That slick lawyer there drew up the note and I made my mark on it in front of witnesses. But, being as how I cain't read, I didn't know just what all was in the writing I put my mark to till these two

Excerpt From THE HIRED GUNS

showed up here the other day and said I'd signed away all my stock to Hoffstatter if I couldn't make my payments on time."

"What kind of a note is this you got Drake to take?" Cimarron asked Butler. "It's been my experience that notes among country folks usually are put together in a fairly slapdash fashion. A few words written on a scrap of paper. A verbal agreement sealed with a handshake. But a note that can let its holder confiscate a man's livestock, well, that's an entirely new kind of critter to me."

"It's called a chattel mortgage," Butler explained. "I have it right here." Butler withdrew a piece of paper from his pocket and handed it to Cimarron.

Cimarron read it and then handed it back. "It looks like they've got you over a barrel, Drake. The note you signed gives Hoffstatter the right to confiscate your stock that's listed on it if you fail to make your payments on time."

"It ain't fair," Mrs. Drake protested in a weak voice. "We allus was able to renew our notes before. Shopkeepers like Deke Masters in the old days, they gave us more time if we had trouble and couldn't pay up on time. Leastaways, that was the way things was before that shyster hit town and Mr. Hoffstatter took over the general store." Mrs. Drake gave the two men she had mentioned a glare that was an angry mixture of contempt and disgust.

"Merrilee's been purty puny of late," Drake declared. "She took sick when we were knee-deep in February, and only now is she starting to get her legs under her again. The doctor bills is what done us in. And we still ain't paid the doc all we owe him. On top of that—look younder at what the drought we've been suffering's gone and done to my two cash crops—my cotton and corn."

Cimarron gazed out over the plowed fields in the distance, they contained shriveled seedlings lying dead in neat rows.

"But I told those two," Drake continued, indicating Butler and Hoffstatter, "that I'd make good on my note if they'd just give me some breathing room. Me and my boy Bobby, we're going to hire on as miners over in the coal fields east of McAlester in Choctaw Nation, and my other boy, Mike, he's hired on at the Carter ranch for the summer. You'll get your money, Hoffstatter. So you can stop hounding me for it with your greedy tongue hanging out like you've been doing."

"If I hadn't of took so poorly—" Merrilee began, but her

Excerpt From THE HIRED GUNS

husband interrupted her with, "It ain't in any way your fault. The Lord sends us trials and it's up to us to grin and bear 'em."

Drake glared again at Butler and Hoffstatter. "But some of the trials He sends sure is mighty hard for even a believer to stomach."

"The fact is, though," Cimarron said solemnly, "Hoffstatter has the right to take your livestock, Drake. That chattel mortgage you made your mark on gives him that right. It's all aboveboard and it has the full force of the law behind it, that agreement does."

"Listed here," Butler said with a smirk as he read from the mortgage in his hand, "are five saddle horses, three yearlings, and two hogs."

"Two of those horses don't even belong to me," Drake protested. "They're my boys'."

"They are, nevertheless, listed here," Butler pointed out, holding up the mortgage agreement.

"But I told you when you was here before I didn't know what it was I was signing," Drake cried. "I thought it was just a promise to pay, like always. You can't take our horses from us and leave us afoot. Me and the boys can't do our jobs if you put us afoot. Should Merrilee take sick again, how can we fetch the doctor or help in a hurry without a horse? And as for those yearlings and hogs, we be depending on them for next winter's meat."

"We'll be taking your stock into town with us now," Butler announced, "and it will all be sold at public auction with the proceeds going to Mr. Hoffstatter. Cimarron, please order these three men to put up their guns and help us gather up the stock."

"Butler and Hoffstatter, they've got the law on their side," Cimarron reluctantly told Drake.

"The law!" Merrilee spat. "The law ought to be out rounding up all the rustlers that have been raising Cain around here instead of tormenting poor folks like us."

"I should have gone and got all our friends to side us," Drake lamented. "I know they'd have been neighborly and stood shoulder to shoulder with me and my family against greedy merchants and shyster lawyers. That's what I should have done."

And that gives me an idea, Cimarron thought an instant before Merrilee shrilled, "No more palavering!"

Excerpt From THE HIRED GUNS

She seized the shotgun from her husband's hands and emptied one of its barrels, blowing Butler's hat from his head. "Now, you three—git or I'll gut-shoot you each and every one!"

Cimarron's Colt had cleared leather an instant after Merrilee had seized her husband's shotgun. Now he leveled it at Drake's heart. "Ma'am, I do advise you and your sons to get rid of your guns so that I won't have to put a bullet in your husband's and their daddy's belly."

As Merrilee swung the shotgun in her hands around toward him, Cimarron continued, "Oh, I know it's likely that you'll be able to ventilate me, considering you've got three guns against this lone one of mine, but I do politely ask you all to consider this. You can shoot me sure enough but I'll guarantee you this: Drake'll be dead before I drop."

For a tense moment there was silence. Merrilee's eyes never blinked. Neither did Cimarron's. Her shotgun remained aimed at him and his .44 remained aimed at her husband.

Then Drake swore volubly. "Put down the gun, Merrilee. You too, boys. They've got us beat, and beat bad. There's just no way around that sad fact."

Merrilee glanced at her husband; then, with evident reluctance, she let the shotgun she was holding slip to the ground. A moment later, Mike Drake dropped his gun. A moment after that, Bobby Drake placed his gun on the ground beside his brother's.

"Now, you three help Butler and Hoffstatter round up the livestock," Cimarron ordered them. He stood his ground as Drake and his two sons began to obey his order, while Merrilee stood motionless and wept the bitter tears of utter and total defeat.

The following afternoon, Cimarron moved through the small crowd that had gathered at a feedlot on the south side of Tullahassee for the auction of the Drake family's livestock. He stopped now and then to speak briefly to a member of the crowd before moving on to someone else.

"The first item on our agenda today, gents," began the corpulent auctioneer a few minutes later as he stood on a wooden crate surveying the crowd, "is those two hogs you see wallowing in that pen yonder. Now, aren't they a mouth-watering sight? They must weigh three hundred or more pounds apiece easy, those two porkers must. They'll go on the block one at a time

Excerpt From THE HIRED GUNS

starting with that one with the real curly tail. Who'll begin the bidding?"

No one in the crowd responded.

The auctioneer's forehead wrinkled in a frown. "I trust you gents have no foolhardy intention of passing up an opportunity to claim as your very own this fine hog I'm offering you. Why, it'll keep a family of five or more in meat from Christmas to Easter with some left over to spare. Let's hear your bids, gents."

"One cent," called out a man in the crowd.

The auctioneer's frown became a scowl. "My ears must be playing me false, gents." He tried a laugh that emerged from his throat as a cackle. "I could have sworn I heard a bid of a single cent, which, as any schoolboy knows, is patently ridiculous for that hog I've got on the block."

"Mr. Auctioneer," Cimarron called up to the man, "your ears aren't telling you lies. That man there, he bid a cent for that hog, and if his bid's not topped, the critter's his. Let's get on with it."

"Who the hell are you?" the auctioneer shot back. "I'll not be goaded—"

"Lawman," Cimarron answered laconically, and held up his star for the auctioneer to see.

"Oh. A deputy marshal. Yes. Well." The auctioneer pulled a polka-dotted handkerchief from his back pocket and swabbed the sweat from his fat face with it. "I have a one-cent bid, gents. Who'll make it five—dollars?"

Silence.

"Going," moaned the auctioneer, "going—"

At the sound of the auctioneer's "Gone," Cimarron glanced over his shoulder at the Drake family, who were standing slightly apart from the crowd, grim expressions on their four faces. He shifted his gaze to the rear of the crowd, where Butler stood beside Hoffstatter, and smiled at the sight of the dismayed looks the two men were exchanging.

The auction continued.

The second hog brought an inital bid of four dollars. But after Cimarron had shouldered his way through the crowd and spoken in low tones to the bidder, the man quickly changed his bid—to one cent.

The auctioneer groaned. Minutes later, the hog was sold for one cent to the man who had changed his bid.

Excerpt From THE HIRED GUNS

Butler and Hoffstatter surged to the front of the crowd. "Stop this farce," Butler demanded at the top of his indignant voice. "We hereby cancel this sale."

Cimarron went up to Butler and clapped a hard hand on the man's skinny shoulder. "This auction's fair and legal, Counselor. And I'm here to see it through to a peaceful conclusion." He patted his gun.

Butler blanched. Hoffstatter swore. And then both men withdrew.

Cimarron signaled to the auctioneer and the sale continued.

In less than ten minutes, all the Drake stock had been purchased by bidders each of whom had bid a cent apiece for the five saddle horses and the three yearlings.

The auctioneer made his way to Hoffstatter and handed the man nine cents. "That's the net proceeds of this sale after I took out my ten percent commission. Next time you fellows decide to foreclose on somebody, you get yourself somebody else to auctioneer the sale of the chattels. My time's worth far more than the measly penny I got out of this deal."

"I don't understand it," Hoffstatter muttered. "Why did everyone—every last bidder—offer only one cent per head of stock?"

"I can answer you that."

Cimarron and the others turned to face Lou Drake, who had just come up to them, trailed by Merrilee and their two sons. "You've got nobody but him"—he pointed to Cimarron—"to thank—or blame, depending upon your point of view—for what happened here today."

"What are you talking about, Drake?" Hoffstatter growled.

"I'm talking about how this here deputy marshal made it his business, I've just been told by a neighbor of mine, to talk to every man jack at the auction. He told them the slick trick you and Butler pulled on me, Hoffstatter. He avowed as how he had to uphold the law by letting you two take my stock, but he swore he weren't going to stand by at the auction and let you fellows have the harvest you were counting on reaping today."

"I haven't the slightest notion of what you're talking about, Drake," Butler stated.

"Get to the point," Hoffstatter demanded.

183

Excerpt From THE HIRED GUNS

"The point," Drake said with a smile, "is that this deputy went and outfoxed you two foxes. He got my friends and neighbors to agree to bid only a single cent for each and every head of my stock that was put on the block. And he also got them to agree to turn the stock they bought back to me, which they've just gladly, they said, gone and done. So it looks like we're right back where we started from."

"You're not, Drake," Cimarron interjected.

"What do you mean, I'm not?" Drake asked warily. "I've got my horses and my other livestock back."

"True. But what I meant is that you've not got Hoffstatter's chattel mortgage to weigh you down. You're free and clear of it now."

"And we do thank you for that, Cimarron," said Merrilee. "If you hadn't've done like you did we'd be in real bad trouble today, but as it is, we're sitting pretty and riding real high."

Cimarron blushed as Merrilee, also blushing, threw her arms around him and kissed him on the cheek.

"Be seeing you, gents," Drake called out to Hoffstatter and Butler, who were striding angrily away.

"Come home and sit to supper with us, Cimarron," Merrilee said.

"I thank you kindly for the invitation, Miz Drake. I'd be real pleased to do that."

Then, as they prepared to drive the stock back to the home place, Cimarron spoke to Drake. "What was it that your wife meant yesterday when she said the law ought to be more concerned about rustlers running loose around here than with chattel mortgages?"

"She meant just what she said. The whole area's infested with rustlers. They range all the way past Choska in the west and farther south than Muskogee. They roam about in Cherokee Nation too—east as far as Tahlequah and Park Hill and farther south than Fort Gibson. Oh, there be a bunch of them, like I said. They're thick as horseflies in May in these parts."

"Are they organized or do they work independent of one another?"

"They stick together like taffy."

"Who ramrods them?"

"Some say it's a rancher name of Dick Haydock, who has a place in a valley about ten miles east of Tullahassee. But don't quote me on that. I wouldn't want no run-in with him."

Excerpt From THE HIRED GUNS

"Have you lost any stock to them?"

"Nope, not me. But that's on account of I'm such small potatoes. They only go after bigger outfits. Men who make a business out of ranching, not sodbusters like me who can barely make ends meet from one week to the next.

"But that's enough talk for now. Let's get this stock of mine legging it for home."

The following morning, after having spent the night with the Drake family, Cimarron thanked them for their warm and obviously genuine invitation to visit them again, bade them all good-bye, and rode away. He wasn't sure of his destination, but he was sure that he was interested in knowing more about the rustlers he had heard about first from Merrilee Drake and then, with more details, from her husband.

Dick Haydock.

The name was a lure dancing invisibly in the air in front of him as he rode on. Drake had said, he recalled, that Haydock was rumored to be the power behind the rustlers. And he had also said that Haydock had a ranch in a valley ten miles east of Tullahassee.

Cimarron turned his horse and rode in an easterly direction, having just made up his mind to pay a visit to Dick Haydock. But he wasn't even halfway to his destination when he spotted two riders herding horses to the south of him. He slowed his black to a walk and pulled his hat down low on his forehead to shield his eyes from the sun.

Two men. Twenty-one horses.

He rode down off the rimrock onto the ground beside a fast-flowing stream.

The riders, when they saw him approaching, put spurs to their mounts. One of the two men yipped loudly to send the herd of horses from a lesiurely lope into a fast gallop.

Looks like they don't encourage company, Cimarron thought as he put heels to his black and went galloping after the group. He caught up with them easily, and asked the bushy-browed and brown-bearded horseman if any of the horses the man and his companion were herding was for sale.

"They're not for sale," the man answered gruffly, his small black eyes alive with an ugly light as he stared steadily at Cimarron. "Is that why you were trailing us? To try to buy a horse?"

185

Excerpt From THE HIRED GUNS

"I've had it in mind for some time to get me another one," Cimarron lied. "So's I could switch from one to the other and that way not be too hard on either one of them. When I saw you two—"

"Let's go, Fitch," said the other man, who was smaller and thinner than his burly companion. "We're wasting time talking to this drifter."

Fitch scratched his stubbled chin, his eyes on Cimarron's black. "Maybe you're wrong about that, Denver. Maybe we're not wasting our time. That there's a sound-looking mount the drifter's perched upon."

Fitch and Denver exchanged glances and then Denver said, "Looks like a big-winded bastard, don't he? I mean the horse."

Cimarron's hand reached for his six-gun, but before he could touch it, both Fitch and Denver had their revolvers unleathered and aimed directly at him. He raised his hands. "You two—you're bent on robbing me of my mount?"

"Step down and cool your saddle," Fitch ordered.

"Horse thieving here in Indian Territory can get you a thousand-dollar fine and fifteen years in prison," Cimarron pointed out.

His warning was ignored. "Fitch told you to light, drifter. Now, do it!"

Reluctantly Cimarron got out of the saddle and stood beside his black with his hands still in the air. "You put a man on foot out here in the middle of nowhere, you could be condemning him to death."

"Whether you live or die's no great concern of ours," Fitch assure him. "Get his horse, Denver."

Denver moved his horse up to the black. He was reaching for the black's reins when the animal suddenly shied and stepped between him and Cimarron. Cimarron quickly unleathered his Colt and fired over the back of his black at Denver.

The man swore as Cimarron's bullet grazed his left shoulder; then he kicked the rump of the black to move it out of his way. Before Cimarron could fire a second time, Denver was barreling toward him.

To avoid being trampled by Denver's mount, Cimarron turned and raced back the way he had come. He fired once over his shoulder at Denver, who, with Fitch right behind him, was riding in swift pursuit. This time he missed his target. He ran on, his heart beginning to pound, and then he dropped down

Excerpt From THE HIRED GUNS

behind a boulder. He propped the butt of his gun on top of the huge stone and, holding it tightly in both hands, took aim at Denver.

Fitch fired at him, his bullet striking the top of the boulder and sending stone dust flying up into Cimarron's eyes. Momentarily blinded, Cimarron wiped his eyes with one hand as tears formed in them. When he could see clearly again, he realized that Fitch and Denver were almost on top of him.

Only one thing to do, he thought, springing to his feet: run for it. He did, heading for some pin oaks in the distance. He never made it to them. Denver cut him off. He quickly changed direction—and almost ran into Fitch, who was bearing down on him fast. He veered again and took the only clear path. As he headed up the sloping rimrock, he got off a fast volley of four shots that failed to slow his pursuers.

Cimarron slowed his pace and glanced over his shoulder. He took aim and fired at Fitch. His gun's hammer clicked on an empty chamber. He tried thumbing cartridges out of his belt, but he was unable to reload his empty .44 and run at the same time.

The edge of the rimrock suddenly came into view directly ahead of him. He tried turning to the left, but Fitch was moving in on him from that side. He turned to the right and saw Denver galloping toward him from that direction. Incredibly, both men were laughing as they closed in behind him. It was their mirthless laughter that told him they had decided not to shoot him. It was the way they were herding him toward the edge of the rimrock that told him they had decided instead to drive him off the cliff.

And then he was there—at the very edge of the rimrock. An instant later, Denver and Fitch forced him to leap from it. Gun still in hand, he went soaring out into empty space. And then he was twisting in midair, turning head over heels, falling fast . . .

About the Author

LEO P. KELLEY was born and raised in Pennsylvania's Wyoming Valley and spent a good part of his boyhood exploring the surrounding mountains, hunting and fishing. He served in the Army Security Agency as a cryptographer, and then went "on the road," working as dishwasher, laborer, etc. He later joined the Merchant Marine and sailed on tankers calling at Texan, South American, and Italian ports. In New York City he attended the New School for Social Research, receiving a BA in Literature. He worked in advertising, promotion, and marketing before leaving the business world to write full time.

Mr. Kelley has published a dozen novels and has several others now in the works. He has also published many short stories in leading magazines.

⊘ SIGNET (0451)

THE OLD WILD WEST

- ☐ THE LAST CHANCE by Frank O'Rourke (115643—$1.95)
- ☐ COLD RIVER by William Judson (137183—$2.75)
- ☐ SIGNET DOUBLE WESTERN: BLOOD JUSTICE & THE VALIANT BUGLES by Gordon D. Shireffs (133390—$3.50)
- ☐ SIGNET DOUBLE WESTERN: BITTER SAGE & THE BUSHWACKERS by Frank Gruber (129202—$3.50)
- ☐ SIGNET DOUBLE WESTERN: QUANTRELL'S RAIDERS & TOWN TAMER by Frank Gruber (127773—$3.50)
- ☐ SIGNET DOUBLE WESTERN: COMANCHE' & RIDE THE WILD TRAIL by Cliff Farrell (115651—$2.50)
- ☐ SIGNET DOUBLE WESTERN: CROSS FIRE & THE RENEGADE by Cliff Farrell (123891—$2.95)
- ☐ SIGNET DOUBLE WESTERN: TROUBLE IN TOMBSTONE & BRAND OF A MAN by Tom Hopkins and Thomas Thompson (116003—$2.50)

Prices slightly higher in Canada

Buy them at your local bookstore or use coupon on next page for ordering.

⓪ SIGNET BOOKS

HOLD ON TO YOUR SADDLE!

(0451)
- ☐ SKINNER, by F.M. Parker. (138139—$2.75)
- ☐ THE GREAT GUNFIGHTERS OF THE WEST, by C. Breihan. (111206—$2.25)
- ☐ LUKE SUTTON: OUTRIDER, by Leo P. Kelley. (134869—$2.50)
- ☐ THE ARROGANT GUNS, by Lewis B. Patten. (138643—$2.75)
- ☐ GUNS AT GRAY BUTTE, by Lewis B. Patten. (135741—$2.50)
- ☐ LAWMAN'S CHOICE by Ray Hogan (112164—$1.95)
- ☐ PILGRIM by Ray Hogan (095766—$1.75)
- ☐ CORUNDA'S GUNS, by Ray Hogan. (133382—$2.50)
- ☐ APACHE MOUNTAIN JUSTICE, by Ray Hogan. (137760—$2.75)
- ☐ THE DOOMSDAY CANYON, by Ray Hogan. (139216—$2.75)

Prices slightly higher in Canada

Buy them at your local bookstore or use this convenient coupon for ordering.

NEW AMERICAN LIBRARY,
P.O. Box 999, Bergenfield, New Jersey 07621

Please send me the books I have checked above. I am enclosing $_____
(please add $1.00 to this order to cover postage and handling). Send check
or money order—no cash or C.O.D.'s. Prices and numbers are subject to change
without notice.

Name _____

Address _____

City _____ State _____ Zip Code _____

Allow 4-6 weeks for delivery.
This offer is subject to withdrawal without notice.

SIGNET WESTERN (0451)

Read all the titles in
THE INDIAN HERITAGE SERIES
by Paul Lederer

☐ **BOOK ONE: MANITOU'S DAUGHTERS**—Manitou was the god of the proud Oneidas, and these were the tribes' chosen daughters: Crenna, the strongest and wisest, who lost her position when she gave herself to the white man; Kala, beautiful and wanton, found her perfect match in the Englishman as ruthless as she; and Sachim, young and innocent, was ill-prepared for the tide of violence and terror that threatened to ravish their lands... Proud women of a proud people—facing the white invaders of their land and their hearts.... (138317—$3.50)

☐ **BOOK TWO: SHAWNEE DAWN**—William and Cara Van der Veghe were raised by their white father and Indian mother deep in the wilderness. But when the tide of white settlement crept closer, William and Cara had to choose sides on the frontier, he with the whites, she with the Shawnee. Brother and sister, bound together by blood, now facing each other over the flames of violence and vengeance.... (138325—$3.50)

☐ **BOOK THREE: SEMINOLE SKIES**—Shanna and her younger sister Lychma were fleeing the invading white men when they fell into even more feared hands—those of the ruthless Seminoles. But Shanna would not be broken, for she had the blood of a princess in her veins. Then she met the legendary warrior, Yui, the one man strong enough to save his people from white conquest—and to turn a woman's burning hate into flaming love.... (122631—$2.95)

Prices higher in Canada.

**Buy them at your local
bookstore or use coupon
on next page for ordering.**

ⓒ SIGNET CLASSIC (0451)

LIFE ON THE FRONTIER

- [ ] **THE OUTCASTS OF POKER FLAT and Other Tales by Bret Harte.** Stories of 19th century Far West and the glorious fringe-inhabitants of Gold Rush California. Introduction by Wallace Stegner, Stanford University. (515943—$2.50)

- [ ] **THE CALL OF THE WILD and Selected Stories by Jack London.** Foreword by Franklin Walker. The American author's vivid picture of the wild life of a dog and a man in the Alaska gold fields. (519949—$1.95)*

- [ ] **LAUGHING BOY by Oliver LaFarge.** The greatest novel yet written about the American Indian, this Pulitzer-prize winner has not been available in paperback for many years. It is, quite simply, the love story of Laughing Boy and Slim Girl—a beautifully written, poignant, moving account of an Indian marriage. (519280—$2.75)*

- [ ] **THE DEERSLAYER by James Fenimore Cooper.** The classic frontier saga of an idealistic youth, raised among the Indians, who emerges to face life with a nobility as pure and proud as the wilderness whose fierce beauty and freedom have claimed his heart. (516451—$2.95)

- [ ] **THE OX-BOW INCIDENT by Walter Van Tilburg Clark.** A relentlessly honest novel of violence and quick justice in the Old West. Afterword by Walter Prescott Webb. (518926—$2.95)*

*Prices slightly higher in Canada.

Buy them at your local bookstore or use this convenient coupon for ordering.

NEW AMERICAN LIBRARY,
P.O. Box 999, Bergenfield, New Jersey 07621

Please send me the books I have checked above. I am enclosing $_____
(please add $1.00 to this order to cover postage and handling). Send check or money order—no cash or C.O.D.'s. Prices and numbers are subject to change without notice.

Name_____

Address_____

City_____State_____Zip Code_____

Allow 4-6 weeks for delivery.
This offer is subject to withdrawal without notice.